The Merriman Chronicles

Book Two

The Threat in the West Indies

Hark, do you hear the sea?
(King Lear : Act 4, Scene 6)
                    - William Shakespeare

Copyright Information

The Merriman Chronicles - Book 2

The Threat in the West Indies

Copyright © 2012 by Roger Burnage

With the exception of certain well known historical figures, the characters in this book have no relation or resemblance to any person living or dead.

All rights reserved. This book and all "The Merriman Chronicles" are works of fiction. No part of this book may be reproduced or used in any manner without written permission of the copyright owner except for the use of quotations in a book review.

Fifth Edition – 2023

Updated by: Robin Burnage
Edited by: Katharine D'Souza

ISBN: 9798871131589 (paperback)
ISBN: 9798871151402 (hardcover)

www.merriman-chronicles.com

Books in the series

James Abel Merriman (1768 – 1843)

A Certain Threat

The Threat in the West Indies

Merriman and the French Invasion

The Threat in the East

The Threat in the Baltic

The Threat in the Americas

The Threat in the Adriatic

The Threat in the Atlantic

Edward James Merriman (1853 - 1928)

The Fateful Voyage

Foreword

In the spring of 1998, workmen demolishing an old nursing home in the country to the north-west of Chester, discovered bundles of old papers concealed behind a bricked-up fireplace. One of the men with more perspicacity than his fellows rescued the papers from the bonfires of rubbish and gave them to his employer, a builder, who, knowing of my interest in such things passed them on to me. The discovered papers were mostly in a very bad state due to the effects of dampness, mildew, and the depredations of vermin over the years, and many of the oldest bundles were totally illegible. Another obvious problem was that the papers had been written by different people and some of the handwriting was not of the best. Sorting the papers into chronological order took many months of part time effort, indeed I gave up on the job for weeks and months at a time, but as I progressed with the work I realised that it was a history of the Merriman family from the late 18th century to the early years of the 20th century.

The first clearly decipherable writings referred to a certain James Abel Merriman, a naval officer at the time of the Napoleonic wars and revealed some startling facts about French activities in and around Ireland and the Irish Sea at that time. I quickly realised that I had in my hands the material for a novel or novels about a little-known part of our history. Other papers showed that besides those serving in the navy, other members of the family were connected with the 22nd Regiment of Foot, the Cheshire Regiment. Intriguingly, a family tree was among the papers in one of the later bundles. Armed with that and from research in local archives, church records etc., it appeared that the last direct male heir of the family, Albert George Merriman was killed in France in 1916 and the last descendant, his unmarried sister Amy Elizabeth, a nurse, was also killed in France in 1917.

Chapter One

Leaving for the West Indies

The year 1793

His Majesty's sloop *Aphrodite* thrashed over the waves, four days out from Portsmouth. Captain James Merriman, a dark-haired man of some twenty two or twenty three years of age, had every reason to be content with the ship and his crew. Indeed, the early morning call of 'Beat to quarters, prepare for action' had been completed in the shortest time yet. The sun was shining, the ship was making good time and, once the Channel had been left behind, no more gales had been met. Captain Merriman walked up and down the small space of the quarter deck and reflected on the last few weeks.

Much had occurred. The action in the Irish Sea and the recovery of the stolen Revenue cutter and its crew of Frenchmen and Irish rebels intent on capturing the Lord Lieutenant of Ireland, Lord Westmorland, at sea, to use him to try and force the government to give up its control of Ireland. Then the capture of the smugglers' own craft and the unfinished fight with the French ship La Sirene. Then he recalled as if it were only yesterday the moment he had asked the delightful Helen to marry him and how pleased he had been when she accepted him. Sorrowfully, he wondered how many months or even years would go by before he saw her again.

He dragged his mind back from that and considered shipboard matters. The pressed men, all smugglers captured in the Irish Sea, were coping well enough; of course, they were seamen, but more used to sailing small fishing smacks. Some of them had been terrified at the prospect of going aloft on the tall masts of the *Aphrodite*. The sharp application of the boatswain's cane to the rumps of the laggards had quickly cured them of that and they were settling in quite well. They had protested violently at first but the reminder that they could have been turned over to the authorities ashore and tried for helping England's enemies soon made them see the error of their ways.

Merriman had pressed them to take the places of his men killed in the fight with the *Sirene*.

"The Admiralty won't worry about that, always desperate for men to fill the King's ships," the Admiral had said, rubbing his hands.

One man though had proved to be a problem, a prodigiously fat man who had been involved with the smugglers and the French in the theft of plumbago mined in Cumberland, used in metal casting, and desperately needed by the French. The spare fat and tallow on the man was rapidly disappearing under shipboard living and extra duties found for him by the First Lieutenant but he was always slow and resentful of following orders.

Damn it, there's still another problem to deal with, thought Merriman. I wonder what has happened to the poor fellow?

He was thinking of Lieutenant Jeavons, originally *Aphrodite's* First Lieutenant, who had suffered a violent blow to the head during the fight with the *Sirene*. Between short periods of lucidity he simply stared into space, not knowing who was speaking to him or where he was.

The surgeon's hopes of an improvement in Jeavons' condition hadn't been realised and Merriman had been obliged to put the man ashore in Plymouth at the newly built Stonehouse hospital on Stonehouse Creek. Lieutenant Colin Laing was now First Lieutenant, David Andrews the second Lieutenant and third Lieutenant was a new man by the name of William Gorman appointed by the Admiral in Portsmouth.

Merriman's thoughts were interrupted by the arrival on deck of Mr Grahame, a tall, lean, hawk-faced individual now bright and breezy with his brief spell of seasickness long past and forgotten. A hard man and unmarried, he worked for the Revenue Service under Lord Stevenage of the Treasury Department which controlled all England's intelligence agents. He was one of England's principal agents. Lord Stevenage was also Merriman's patron. They had met when Merriman and his crew saved the passengers on an Indiaman which was being attacked by Algerian corsairs.

"Good morning, James," said Grahame. "A lovely morning and we are making good progress I think." He paused. "Perhaps we could have a few minutes conversation in your cabin?"

Merriman knew what it would be about. He was the ship's Captain and responsible for all aspects of the ship's safety and handling but when and where the ship went was under Grahame's orders. A good working relationship had been forged between them during the events in the Irish Sea but so far Grahame had not told him his plans for when they arrived in the West Indies.

When they were settled with cups of coffee prepared by Merriman's servant Peters who then promptly disappeared into his own little space, Grahame began.

"I haven't discussed with you exactly what we are to do in the West Indies, James. I'm sorry about that but I have been considering the options open to us. I have a list of several agents on various islands, both English and French, some I consider to be trustworthy and some not. Many may not be even alive. Of course, as you know, many of them only do it for the money but we can discover much of the French activities on the islands. What I learn from the first people I see will decide our own actions, which islands we visit first and so on, although I believe Jamaica will be the most important."

"We must call at Bridgetown in Barbados first, sir, it's the first port of call where we can obtain fresh water which is plentiful there," said Merriman. "And I want to keep up our supplies, who knows when we shall have another opportunity. I also have dispatches and letters for the Admiral in command."

"Very well, James. Tell me what you know about Barbados, I have no dependable agents there. What I do know I have only read about but I understand that it has been an English possession since 1655 and exports were sugar, rum, indigo and ginger, grown mostly by white labour, but since the plantations of cotton and tobacco have expanded more black slaves are used.

Devilish bad business the slave trade, not what England should be involved in, it should be abolished," remarked Grahame. "Have there been any slave uprisings there as in other places?"

"I agree with your sentiments, sir, I would like to see an end to that trade, and I have heard that some people in Parliament are trying to bring that about but without much success. Too many people with vested interests in the sugar trade. As to slave revolts I don't know, but I heard about a hurricane in 1780 which killed thousands of people there and destroyed many of the plantations. Mr Cuthbert the Master tells me that we should anchor in Carlisle Bay in the south of the island which is a good harbour except in bad weather, otherwise it would have become our major naval base in the Caribbean with plenty of good clean water."

"All right. I will take the opportunity to go ashore and find out more. Have they a garrison big enough to hold the island if there is any trouble with the slaves? France has little naval force over there now, so I don't think we have to worry about them on that score just yet. I must see if there is anybody there that I might recruit into my network to pass on anything he might learn about any French activities of course, or even Spanish activities. The Frogs are very good at causing unrest amongst the slaves on many islands which is one reason we are here."

Merriman nodded his agreement.

"I know you must report our presence to the Admiral in command," Grahame went on, "but after that I would like to visit some of the other islands in the chain up to Antigua. In Antigua there is one man I must see before we sail further north. He is a general merchant from Bristol. All his trading ships were taken by the French, meaning he hates them and would do anything to discomfit them. After the loss of his ships, he moved to Antigua and started business as an agent dealing in sugar, tobacco, coffee, and such. Quite successfully I believe, and he now has two new ships. In his position he meets many other traders and ships' masters, from whom hears a lot of news, gossip, and information which he passes on to us. There are some others there I must try and see."

"There should be no problem with that, sir. As you know we are carrying bags of mail for the garrison there and dispatches for the Admiral. The problem may be the various other Admirals I must report to. Each of them will want the *Aphrodite* to come under his command as he is nominally in command of all naval vessels in his area. He won't be best pleased that we have letters from the Admiralty and the First Minister Mr Pitt urging him and all persons of authority to give us all the essential help that we think that we may need."

"It may be for the best, James, to impress on him the importance of our mission. I have the full weight of the Government behind me which should stifle any objections."

The two men returned to the quarterdeck and the watch keeping officers and men moved over to the lee side in time honoured convention. The Officer of the Watch, Mr Andrews touched his hat and reported the ship's condition to his captain. Every member of the crew knew that the captain's eye would see any fault with the ship and would miss nothing, but Merriman knew that the skies would fall before Lieutenants Laing and Andrews missed anything for their captain to notice.

Their conversation then became more general. Mr Graham commented that the crew seemed happy enough with the weather conditions, no wet clothes to worry about; in fact, it was ideal for an Atlantic cruise.

"Yes, sir, Jack is happy enough for now certainly but perhaps you haven't experienced a real Atlantic gale. Things can change so rapidly out here you wouldn't believe it."

"How are the new men shaping up, James? I haven't seen any trouble, has there been any?"

"No, sir, nothing more than a few grumbles but they have settled into the ship's routine well enough."

And so, the days passed as the ship headed southwards, routine maintenance on the ship continued and very quickly they were only a few days from the point where they could expect to meet the North-east trade winds, the starting point for the voyage across the Atlantic, a voyage of some three thousand miles.

Merriman and his officers exercised every day at swordplay under the instruction of Lieutenant St James, the marine officer, who was an accomplished swordsman. They were all improving, even the midshipmen, and St James reminded them often of the phrase from Cowper's work: *No skill in swordsmanship, however just, can be secure against a madman's thrust'.* The crews were also improving their ability with swords with daily practice.

Merriman decided to invite all the officers to dinner, something he had not yet done, so that he could inform them about the nature of the ship's duties in the West Indies. He beckoned Mr Oakley, the midshipman of the watch who nearly tripped over a ring-bolt in his haste to obey.

"Mr Oakley, I appreciate your eagerness to discover what I want done but you really must learn to place your feet more carefully and not dash about like an excited puppy. After all you are an officer and must show the decorum required. Now then, I want you to call on all the officers, not forgetting Mr Cuthbert and Mr McBride, to tell them that they are all invited for dinner tonight; except the duty watch of course. Oh, and pass the word for the cook to come aft right away."

"Aye-aye, sir," exclaimed the boy, dashing off and nearly crashing into a seaman who was standing behind him binding a rope's end.

Merriman shook his head and smiled to himself at the youth's impetuosity. The ship's cook duly appeared, looking worried in case he had done something wrong, but Merriman simply informed him that one of his own pigs was to be killed and prepared for the officer's dinner later. "Mark you, Cook, I want plenty of crackling on it and we have a few apples left which you can use to make sauce."

Chapter Two

Officers told about the ship's orders

It was a small but convivial gathering in Merriman's quarters that evening whilst Lieutenant Andrews kept the watch on deck with Midshipman Shrigley. Mr Grahame, Lieutenants Laing, Gorman, and St James the marine officer, Mr Cuthbert the sailing master, Mr Oakley the midshipman and the ship's surgeon Mr McBride were there. They were making heavy inroads into Merriman's wine chest, although McBride restricted himself to only one glass, having had problems with alcohol in the past.

Looking round the table, Merriman again reflected how lucky he was to have such a good set of officers and a willing and competent crew. Unconsciously he squeezed a small, tightly bound ball of rags with his left hand as his doctor had told him to do after the operation to remove fragments from the wound in his arm, received in the fight with the corsairs.

"It will strengthen the muscles, James," the doctor had said. Since then, he had always carried it about his person and was often seen walking on deck, squeezing it without really noticing what he was doing.

"Does your arm still bother you, sir?" asked a greatly daring Andrews.

"Not too much now but it has become a habit to squeeze this damned ball," said Merriman thrusting it into a pocket as the cook and Peters brought the meal into the cabin. "Now then, gentlemen, remember this quote: *'Now good digestion wait on appetite and health on both'*. That is from Shakespeare's Macbeth, I believe."

"Indeed, it is, Captain, and Cicero said something similar, but I can't call it to mind," said Grahame.

"Sir, I think it is: *'Live not to eat but eat to live'*," said young Oakley.

Both Merriman and Grahame had each discovered in the other a pleasure in finding apt sayings or Shakespearian quotations and now they both stared at Oakley in amazement. "Are you interested in Cicero, young man?" asked Grahame.

"No, not really, sir. Some quotations were drilled into us at school but most of them are gone now."

Over the meal the conversation drifted to their recent experiences in Dublin and the trial of the rebels. All of the officers had been heartily welcomed by Dublin society and all invited to dances and dinners, especially by ladies with unmarried daughters. The events quickly began to pall and a reluctance to accept invitations became apparent. The marine officer St James, who had always been the centre of a group of young ladies with his arm in a sling and playing the part of the wounded hero to perfection, had put it into words. "Daren't go ashore again, sir, I'll find myself up at the altar if I do. I had no idea of the lengths some girls would go to, to trap a fellow. A kiss and a squeeze behind the drapes seems little enough but one loses interest even in that when the girl's mother is sighted bearing down like a frigate under full sail." The other men had agreed.

"Ye gods," exclaimed Laing a quiet half hour later. "The cook has really excelled himself this time, sir. That crackling is the best I have eaten for years." He stifled a prodigious belch, and smiled. "My grandmother made marvellous crackling," he said dreamily, obviously remembering pork crackling of his youth, before asking, "Is that piece going begging?"

There were more expressions of pleasure as Merriman's man Peters cleared the table and produced crackers and a large piece of cheese. When all that had been cleared, Merriman said, "Mr Oakley, what must you do?"

"Yes, sir, sorry sir, I must propose the loyal toast."

After that had been proposed by Mr Oakley, with the officers standing crouched down as the low headroom demanded, Merriman called for silence. "Gentlemen, Mr

McBride has some information for us concerning our forthcoming visit to the West Indies."

"Thank you, sir. Gentlemen, I am sure that most of you have heard about or even seen the effects of that dreaded scourge Scurvy. On long voyages it kills more men than enemy action and until recently it was not known what caused it. It seems that a Naval surgeon, James Lind, a Scotsman I am pleased to say, has studied the matter closely and proved that it can be prevented or cured by the use of citrus fruit - oranges, lemons, or limes as part of a seaman's diet. Back in 1753 he produced a treatise on this subject but only now is the Admiralty beginning to wake up and take notice of it."

He paused for a sip of wine before going on. "Some of you will remember Dr Simpson who saved Mr Grahame's life some weeks ago after the affair in the Irish Sea. He has studied this problem and has lent to me a copy of Lind's writings in the hope it will help us. He also passed on to me his notes about health problems in tropical areas so I am very hopeful that I can keep us all healthy."

"Thank you, Mr McBride, we all look to you in this matter but there are certain other things we can do," said Merriman. "You know that the worst problems in the Indies are Yellow Fever and Dysentery. They have killed thousands, nearly half of our troops in various garrisons often within twelve months of their arrival. Another killer is locally brewed rum, it's cheap and readily available and rather foul. Therefore, we must be sure to prevent any being bought from boat traders when we are in port. All parts of the ship are to be as well-ventilated as possible at all times and only essential contact will be made ashore. Mr St James, your marines must do all they can to keep local traders away. If warnings won't do it, a musket shot into the bottom of the boat should do it or maybe even a round shot dropped in will."

"Aye aye, sir," replied the marine officer. "The men would probably relish dropping a shot onto them."

"Now then, gentlemen," continued Merriman, "our visit to Barbados will be a short one, just long enough to take on more water and as much fresh fruit as you, Mr McBride, decide is necessary and for me to make a courtesy call on the Admiral."

"Don't we have a treaty with Portugal, sir?" asked young Oakley.

"Indeed, we do," said Grahame. "It has been in existence since 1386 or thereabouts. It's called the Windsor Treaty, must be one of the oldest in existence and still holding today, but that is the Azores you are thinking about, not Barbados, although I have no doubt that we would be welcome in the Azores if we stopped there but we do not plan to do so."

Chapter Three

Traitors leave England on a Slave Ship

Four weeks before *Aphrodite* left Plymouth, two men bartered with the captain of a trading ship in Liverpool for passage to the Americas. It was settled, but it was obvious to the captain that they were in a hurry to get away. The two men were unshaven and dishevelled, and he wondered what the bigger man carried in the bag he clutched tightly. No doubt they were fugitives from the law. But the captain was an unsavoury rogue and he thought there may be more money in the bag than they had agreed to pay him. Once at sea, the two men were overpowered while the captain and some rough-looking seamen seized the bag to find out what was in it. More than money, there were jewels carefully wrapped in various items of clothing and a lawyer's wig which caused great amusement among the crew.

The captain glared balefully at the two wretched men. "You are escaping from the law, I expect, and there may be a reward out for you," he said. "But these jewels are probably worth more than any reward, so I'll keep them. Now tell me about yourselves. You, fat man, you must be a lawyer, otherwise why do you have a wig? Come on, out with it, why do you want to leave England? Tell me before I throw you overboard."

"Yes, I am a lawyer," stammered the frightened man. "My name is Jerimiah Robinson, and this is my clerk, Beadle. We stole the jewels from my wife, the bitch, she demanded more and more money and I was driven to theft to satisfy her. So, we beat her, badly, she may be dead for all I know, and we decided to try our luck in America. We paid you and you said you would take us there."

"Yes, I did, didn't I? Well I will but not directly, we are taking a detour round to the Bight of Benin in Africa to barter with coastal tribes for their prisoners who we'll take to America and Jamaica and sell as slaves. So, I've decided that you'll work your passage and work hard you will, or maybe I'll sell you as slaves or throw you to the sharks."

Later, lying in a stinking hammock, Robinson cursed everybody and himself for the bad luck which had followed him. If his wife had not herself been so greedy then he would not have agreed to carry letters from Ireland to France in the course of legal business. He had been very well paid and only months later had he realised that they were between Irish rebels and French agents. That made him and Beadle traitors and he was glad he had said nothing of that to the captain. He groaned at the thought of the weeks of hard toil ahead of him.

Chapter Four

Battle with Privateers

Aphrodite continued her journey westward across the Atlantic Ocean. Merriman had originally thought of calling in at Punto Delgado in the Azores to collect a large number of oranges and lemons, enough to give each member of the crew more than half a fruit each per day. Bearing in mind the advice of the ship's surgeon, he was insistent that everybody had the fruit, enjoining the petty officers to ensure that each man ate his portion with no shirkers. This however proved unnecessary as it was obvious that the men enjoyed the sweet fruit when they got it. With time pressing though, he reluctantly decided to wait until they arrived in Barbados.

Some days later, one of the lookouts aloft yelled, "Deck there, topmasts on the horizon dead ahead." Merriman immediately ordered the ship to action stations.

After a short while the thud of gunfire was heard over the clatter of partitions and furniture being taken down to the hold.

Merriman gave the order, "Up you go with your glass, Mr Gorman and tell me what you see."

Lieutenant Gorman, climbing like a monkey, was quickly at the mainmast crosstrees and shouting, "It's a small convoy heading north, sir. It looks to be under attack." He waited a few more minutes, then shouted excitedly, "There's an English frigate, sir. I can see her colours, seems to be heavily engaged with some small, fast sloops. And there's another smaller ship, sir, a brig, fighting the sloops."

"I will have our colours hoisted, Mr Laing, and you can bring Mr Gorman down to his station at the guns." Merriman waited until the action could be seen from the deck though gun smoke obscured the ships until the wind took it away. As the ship drew closer, he said, "I'll have the courses off her right away, Mr Laing and have the guns loaded with round shot and run out. Those sloops must be privateers and full of men."

After Laing bawled out the orders, Merriman was pleased to see the guns hauled into position and the gun ports rise as one as the ship showed her teeth, whilst the lower mainsails - the courses - disappeared like magic. As the noise and bustle died down, Merriman looked along the length of his ship. Every man was in his position, including the powder boys, all looking eager for the fight to come. The marines were up in the fighting tops or at the hammock nettings with muskets at the ready and officers Andrews and Gorman were at their positions by their divisions of guns larboard and starboard. Lieutenant Laing was on the quarterdeck near him with Midshipman Oakley while Midshipman Shrigley was by his flag lockers at the stern.

Only moments later they were in the thick of it. Merriman steered *Aphrodite* directly at the closest privateer which was stern on to *Aphrodite*. They did not seem aware of the threat until too late. He waited until his ship was almost alongside before he ordered, "Open fire, Mr Laing." Every gun of the starboard battery spoke together with clouds of smoke obscuring the target until they were clear.

As the smoke cleared, Merriman looked back. The privateer had been badly damaged, holed amidships, and was already listing heavily to one side. As he watched, the mainmast crashed down.

"Well done, sir. That'll teach them," crowed Laing.

Shrigley was capering about with excitement and there were cheers from the crew as they reloaded the guns in moments. Merriman was looking ahead to see the stern of the brig with one of the privateers alongside on its starboard side and the crew fighting desperately to stop the flood of boarders, with another sloop closing from ahead on the other side.

"We'll engage that other sloop next, Mr Laing. We'll pass between it and the brig and give them the larboard broadside first to slow her down, then we'll go about and give her another broadside before we go about again and deal with the one alongside the brig."

As Laing bawled the necessary orders, Merriman turned as his man Owen appeared with his sword saying, "I brought this, sir, thought you might need it."

The larboard side broadside erupted doing enormous damage to the sloop; scores of men must have been killed or wounded because the privateers always carried plenty of men ready to form prize crews of captured ships. But *Aphrodite* did not escape as easily as she had done with the first sloop.

This second privateer had time to prepare and fired her broadside almost at the same time and, although her weight of shot was not as heavy as that of *Aphrodite,* it did do damage. Splinters flew in all directions causing some casualties; one gun was upended onto a screaming sailor and Merriman saw a marine thrown back with blood pouring from his throat. Then, before they were fully past, Laing's bellowed orders had men hauling madly on the braces and sheets to bring the ship round onto the other tack. *Aphrodite* seemed to spin on the spot and as she passed the privateer again a second broadside was delivered, wreaking havoc and bringing down her mainmast with little fire in return.

"Round to larboard, Mr Laing. We'll go round astern of the brig and give the other fellow a broadside along the length of him." As they passed round the stern and the privateer ship appeared, Merriman shouted, "Mr Andrews, fire as your guns bear. Mr Laing, have the boarding parties ready."

One by one the guns erupted in smoke and flame, the shot bursting in at the stern and tearing along the length of the unfortunate ship, doing immense damage, and killing many men before *Aphrodite* turned and crashed against the side of it. Merriman, sword in hand, leapt across the gap followed by his boarding party with Lieutenant Gorman leading his party from the forecastle. There was little resistance from the privateers left alive, they threw down their weapons and meekly surrendered.

The brig's crew were cheering wildly as they boarded the ship and the commander of the brig came forward to shake Merriman's hand saying, "Congratulations, sir, I thought we were done for when we saw those two closing, one astern and the other on our larboard side. It looked as though they wanted to dispose of us before tackling the merchant ships. I'm Lieutenant Humphreys, sir, Captain of this ship. Please accept my congratulations and thanks again. The way you dealt with them all, privateers the lot, was good to see." He looked about him at the carnage on the brig's deck. "We've lost some good men, but I believe we will manage to clear up and get back to the convoy."

"I'm glad we were in time to help, Mr Humphries. Fortunately, both of us can make up for our losses from the prisoners. Press as many as you need, some will be French or even Americans, but the Admiralty won't worry. I leave it to you to sort them out and I'll take three of them. I trust your wound is not too serious, sir?" The man was bleeding profusely from a head wound, indeed the shoulder of his coat was sodden with blood and he swayed on his feet. "Owen, pass the word for Mr McBride to come over at once to look to the wounded over here." He turned back to Humphries saying, "We have an excellent surgeon aboard, sir, he and his assistants will soon have you and your men set to rights."

"Thank you, sir, we have a doctor of sorts, but I think this may be too much for him. But what about your own crew, have you no casualties?"

Merriman replied, "We sustained some damage, sir, but less than I expected. A few men wounded and two men killed."

"What has happened to the privateers now?" asked Humphries. "I know that of the two you engaged one sank and the other is badly damaged."

They looked around to see that there were indeed only two still afloat, the dismasted one and also the one tied alongside the brig.

"Well, I don't think you will be bothered with them again, Mr Humphreys. The one alongside is a wreck, surprising that she's still afloat. I would advise you to have it cut adrift before it drags you over."

A hail from the mast head cut across their conversation, "Deck there, *Vigilant* is approaching, sir." The man pointed, and sure enough the frigate was rapidly closing with them and then hove to a hundred yards away with the officers and men cheering at the victory. There was no sign of the privateers the frigate had been fighting.

A string of flags appeared on the frigate and Shrigley reported, "Frigate signals us, sir, Captains to report to *Vigilant* immediately."

Merriman looked down at his blood-splashed uniform and that of Humphreys. Neither of them was ready to see a senior officer. "The signal said immediately, Mr Humphreys, I shall have to go as I am, but let Mr McBride look to your head first and then I'll send the boat back for you." Leaving orders to his officers, Merriman was hastily rowed across to the *Vigilant.*

Signs of battle were evident. Damaged rigging, which was being repaired, and some wounded men, but the most distressing sight was the small group of bodies lined up ready for burial at sea. Merriman saw it all as he was taken down to the captain's cabin.

"I assume you are the captain of the sloop, sir? Welcome aboard, Lieutenant… my apologies, Captain I see. You'll join me in a glass of wine I hope, and where is Mr Humphries, not hurt, I hope?" asked the captain, Gordon by name.

Merriman hastily introduced himself and told him that Humphries had been wounded but would come over as soon as the surgeon had seen to him. As the captain's servant lifted a bottle from a magnificent silver wine chest and dispensed the drinks, Merriman quickly looked around him noting how much bigger the frigate's cabin was than his own aboard *Aphrodite*. That the captain was wealthy and married was quite obvious. The furniture was of far better quality than the dockyards supplied and the curtains, though much faded, showed a woman's touch.

"Your health, Captain Merriman," said Captain Gordon. "Your arrival was unexpected but very welcome. This convoy sailed from Barbados keeping well out to sea, more eastward than usual expecting to turn north to north-east once well away from land in the hope of avoiding interception by the damned privateers. As you saw, that hope was shattered and we encountered ten of them. Thanks to you they have been defeated. *Vigilant* sank two and battered two more, you and Mr

Humphries accounted for another three and the others fled. Maybe we can reach England without any more bother. But you know, I think there must be a spy in the Admiral's offices because our plan was only talked about there and none of the convoy captains knew about it until we were on the point of sailing. Now then, tell me what your orders are, but before that I must comment on your ship, one of the new sort of sloops I think, but it is the first I have seen with three masts and such big square sails. Sails well, does she?"

"Indeed she does, sir, she is more like a small frigate really, fast and I am constantly amazed at how far up to the wind she will sail. As to why I am heading to Antigua, sir, I cannot divulge any details, but I think these documents will show my *bona fides.*"

He handed over his Admiralty orders and the letter from Mr Pitt. The captain's eyebrows rose as he read them. "Very good, sir," he said. "It is obviously an important mission that you are on so I won't detain you any longer than necessary, but my report to the Admiralty will contain favourable mention of this encounter."

"Thank you, sir," Merriman replied courteously, about to speak of the action when they were interrupted by the arrival of Humphries, very pale and with a heavy bandage round his head.

"My dear fellow, you look terrible," said Gordon. "Sit down right away. A glass of wine perhaps?"

"Thank you, sir, that I would like." Humphries paused briefly to accept a glass then continued, "This wound is not too bad, but I lost a lot of blood." He turned to Merriman and said, "Your surgeon fixed me up and said it would heal quickly, sir."

"Good, good, I'm pleased to hear it," said Captain Gordon. "Will you be able to continue our voyage?"

"Oh yes, sir, I'm a little weak but well able to carry on."

Merriman spoke up, "Another thing, sir, are you aware that France declared war on us in January, which is in part the reason for my orders?"

"By God! No! Doesn't surprise me though, I have been expecting it. Whilst I relish the thought of action, I hope it won't amount to anything serious as this ship is riddled with worms and is as likely as not to fall apart if we fire too many broadsides. She's an old ship, never been copper bottomed, which is the main reason I'm escorting the convoy back to England. Maybe she will be scrapped but that is for the dockyard to say."

"Thank you for your hospitality, sir, and may I wish you a safe voyage?"

"Indeed, you may and success to you too, sir," responded Captain Gordon as Merriman made his way back to his boat.

Aphrodite was soon on her way and the convoy's masts disappeared below the horizon.

Chapter Five

Arrival at Barbados

On arrival at Barbados, Merriman and Grahame lost no time in going ashore at Bridgetown to see the Rear Admiral commanding, Sir Henry Bartlett. His flag was flying over a large building instead of his flagship and he quickly explained why to them. "Cooler here, gentlemen, with all windows and doors open, and you will have noticed that we are well shaded for most of the day by palm trees."

Merriman and Grahame showed the Admiral the orders and other documents and informed him of their requirements.

"Well, gentlemen, I doubt I can help you much. I have only recently arrived, but I do know we are well placed to defend ourselves if necessary. As to French agents I'm sure there must be some, but I have seen or heard nothing suspicious. Certainly, my predecessor told me nothing of such matters."

"Thank you, sir, perhaps if you find out anything you could send news to me in Antigua which I will make my base for further enquiries around the islands?" Grahame said.

"Certainly, I will Mr Grahame, there are still plenty of small English trading ships coming and going between the islands, I'm sure that one or two could be persuaded to carry messages. Also, I will question the captains to see if they can tell us anything which will be of use to you. As you know, Barbados has been British since sixteen twenty seven, going on for nearly two centuries and we are very well established and plentiful producers of tobacco, cotton, indigo and ginger. There are many slaves of course but they are quite well looked after by the owners and overseers and there have been no reports of any recent unrest."

"Do you know, sir, what conditions are like in the Leeward and Windward Islands? Most of them have been fought over by the French, Spanish and ourselves for years but we are unsure who owns which at the present time?" asked Merriman. "We don't want to find ourselves prisoners because we unknowingly entered an enemy port."

The Admiral's brow creased in thought. "I can only tell you what I know, the situation is quite fluid although it will soon change in our favour. Starting at the southern end, the Windward Islands, Trinidad and Tobago are Spanish. I don't know about the smaller islands, but they are divided from the Leeward Islands by St Lucia and Martinique which are French, as is Guadeloupe. We have Montserrat and our biggest asset Antigua. Most of Hispaniola is divided between the French and Spanish who are always fighting. Of course, we have Jamaica, but again I have no knowledge about the smaller islands. And now, gentlemen, perhaps you will be my guests at dinner this evening?"

"I regret not, sir, but thank you for the invitation. I hope the situation here will remain quiet, but after fresh watering is finished, we must be on our way southward to Trinidad and Tobago from where we must work our way back up the chain of islands to Antigua and see if there is any news there about any French activity." They left with mutual expressions of goodwill and the *Aphrodite* was quickly on her way.

"All seemed to be satisfactory there, sir," remarked Merriman as Barbados fell astern.

"Indeed so," replied Grahame, "but it may be different in Trinidad and Tobago. They are owned by France at present, but I don't think it will be long before we take them back. They have all changed hands several times but there will be a lot of French sympathy still there. There was a slave uprising only two years ago in St Vincent, doubtless promoted by French revolutionary agents, but it was crushed. I believe Grenada is still ours, but what we will find there I don't know."

Despite calling at multiple places on their onward journey, there was no contact with the agents who were supposed to be there and so no fresh news of French or Spanish agents. So they left and headed north, but not before asking the Governors and military commanders in the British owned islands to send word to Barbados or Antigua of anything new.

Chapter Six

Death in St Lucia

Grahame and Merriman sat below with the inevitable cups of coffee as they approached the southern end of St Lucia.

"We mustn't sail too close yet, James. I shall go ashore there under the cover of darkness. We have a very good man there by the name of George Briggs, or at least we had. Nothing has been heard from him since the French took the island and I fear for his safety. I know where he lives, quite near to the shore on the south side of the island."

Merriman frowned. "That is going to be risky, sir. The French will have patrols all over the place not to mention local people with French sympathies who would tell the army about you."

"Nonetheless I must go. If I can be taken ashore at an hour or two before midnight that will give me plenty of time to find Briggs and for you to take me off again before dawn."

Fortunately it was a dark night, the moon was completely obscured by dark clouds as *Aphrodite* crept towards the shore and silently anchored. The smallest boat was lowered and Grahame, dressed in dark clothing, was rowed ashore. It took him a little while to orientate himself, the two big trees he was looking for had been reduced to only one, but he was soon walking inland as quietly as he could, listening for anything unusual. He recognised the solitary cottage belonging to Briggs and moved stealthily forward towards a lighted window. The sound of loud voices inside warned him and he peered cautiously in. Three roughly dressed soldiers were sitting round a table scattered with empty wine bottles while a fourth sprawled on a rough bed, fast asleep. None of them was Briggs. Grahame knew that he was neat and tidy in his habits and if he were still living there, he would never have let the place get in such a state.

Grahame realised that he could do nothing there, but after a little thought, he decided to investigate further. He had been aware as he approached the cottage that there was a foul smell coming from somewhere behind the cottage. *It's death, somebody or something has died,* he thought. He found a small barn with the door wide open. A man's body was hanging from the beam above the door and had been for some time it seemed due to the smell of putrefying flesh. There was just enough light to see the man in more detail and Grahame gasped in horror. He had a rough wooden peg sticking out below his trouser leg and Grahame knew immediately that it was Briggs hanging there.

Sadly, he shook his head but then, warned by the scrape of a door opening, he silently moved deeper into the shadows. A man appeared carrying a small lantern but all he wanted to do was relieve himself. After standing facing the wall for what seemed like more than five minutes he grunted and went back inside. Grahame quietly returned to the path and was soon on the beach. He had a small lantern and lit it so he was able to flash a signal seaward. The small boat appeared from the darkness and in no time he was back aboard the ship.

"My dear, sir, you look awful, what happened to you?" asked Merriman once they were in his cabin. "Here, Peters, some brandy for Mr Grahame, quickly now."

Grahame drank the brandy in one long draught and said, "I needed that, James. It was horrible. Briggs is dead, had been for many days judging by the state of his body and French soldiers are billeted there. But I must go back again tomorrow night, Briggs was a careful man and good at what he did. I know he would have hidden any notes he made, and I know where. I couldn't get to them because of the soldiers so I will need a few of your best men to dispose of them. Perhaps you have some erstwhile poachers in your crew, men who can move quietly at night and won't mind killing some drunken, murdering Frenchmen. Five or six men should be enough for the job. And now, James, we should move away to sea."

Merriman smiled. "All taken care of, sir, we shall be far enough away from land and out of sight by daylight. And now may I suggest that you get some sleep if you are going ashore again later."

So, led by Grahame, a small party of hardened men including ex-poacher Jackson were set ashore where Grahame had landed previously. Jackson had been told what to look for and sent ahead but he quickly returned, "Found the big tree, sir, 'an I went further 'till I could see the cottage. Couldn't miss it, sir, lot of noisy drunken singing and shouting coming from it."

"Well done. Now the rest of you, we'll creep closer, quietly mind, until we can see if there are still only four men in there." They did so and Grahame peeped in. "Right, men, there are five of them now, all drunk I think so it should be easy to dispose of them. No gunfire, we don't want to alert any more French who may be nearby."

It was ridiculously easy. The *Aphrodite's* crew poured through the door and most of the French died before their fuddled brains realised what was happening. Cold steel did the work and the only one who tried to resist was a sergeant not as drunk as the rest, but a cutlass thrust into his chest soon stretched him out on the floor.

Grahame, who had not taken part in the killing, carefully stepped over the blood and bodies to the pull a rough wooden cupboard away from the wall by the stone fireplace. It revealed a section of stonework with one stone of a slightly different colour. Grahame borrowed a cutlass, thrust it in a narrow gap next to that stone and slowly managed to lever the stone out. Thrusting his arm inside the void he pulled out a small metal box and a thick wad of paper.

"That's what we came for. Now, I want to do one more thing, I want the body hanging in the barn buried. He was a good man and served England well."

It was soon done; a spade was found in the barn and the sailors swiftly cut down and buried the body. Once again, on the beach a quick flash of the lantern brought the boat in and very soon they were back aboard the ship.

Chapter Seven

Spying in Martinique

The next day found the ship well away from sight of any island and slowly moving north towards Martinique, the French held island. Merriman and Grahame had spent some time reading the hastily scrawled notes left by Briggs, and found much information about the forts and location of troops. In the little metal box, they found a short note asking the finder to notify his daughter of his death and to give her a pretty necklace left with it which had been her mother's.

"I will see to that, her address in England is also here," said Grahame. "I will do it as soon as I reach England. I will not forget."

They sat quietly for a few moments, then Grahame said, "James, I have more to tell you. I was born in Martinique; my parents had a small plantation there and we lived with my aunt and uncle. As a boy I roamed all over the island and I know it very well except for some of the thickest forest to the north. Anyway, when my mother died, my father left the plantation to his brother and took me back to England, where he sent me to Oxford, as he said to turn me into a proper gentleman instead of a ragamuffin. I suppose that worked, for I came to the attention of Lord Stevenage and joined the Treasury service soon after. I have been involved with this spying business for over twenty years now and find I quite enjoy it, although I think I'm getting a bit too old for it now."

"Nonsense, sir, you are as fit as I am. I'm sure you have many more years ahead of you yet."

"Kind of you to say so, James, but I know what I can and cannot do. And I have a longing to see Martinique again. Anyway, my aunt and uncle may be able to tell me much about the French army there. We have corresponded occasionally so I think they will give me shelter although they are now getting on in years. So, James, I want you to set me ashore as before, I'll tell you where and I may be there two or three days. The island is only five miles or so wide going west from Fort Royal and there is a small, secluded cove on the east coast which should be suitable, I fished there as a boy. The old plantation is only a few miles inland from there, roughly in the middle of the island."

"Do you propose to go alone, sir? The place will be alive with French soldiers, patrols and camps and forts. Perhaps you should take one or two men with you to help."

"Nonsense, James, I know the island well, all the small tracks between villages and plantation buildings and farms. It will have changed somewhat from when I was there but I'm certain I can find my way, and I speak French fluently as you know. Remember the line from Romeo and Juliet, James - *'I have night's cloak to hide me from their sight'.*"

"Well then, sir, if I can't change your mind, we had better start the arrangements. First of all, can you show Mr Cuthbert and myself where on the chart you want to land?"

Later, the *Aphrodite* kept well out of sight of land until it was dark and then slowly approached the place Grahame thought he had to land. The longboat was launched, and a small swivel gun mounted in the bows in case of trouble when landing. When word went round the ship that Mr Grahame was going ashore there was no end of volunteers to go in the boat, but Merriman selected men he knew to be reliable and steady including Owen, his cox'n, Jackson, the Sergeant and three marines. All the men were armed but only the marines carried loaded muskets, the sergeant offering severe punishment for any man foolishly discharging his musket without orders.

At the last moment, Merriman announced that he was going as well. "Mr Laing, the ship is yours, try not to lose it," he said, knowing full well that his First Lieutenant was fully capable.

When all were in the boat he entered last, as was his due, and the boat pushed off. Oars had been muffled with greasy rags round the rowlocks and all of them except the oarsmen crouched in the bottom of the boat. Merriman and Grahame stayed together going over the details once more. He was worried that he may not see Grahame again, so he ensured that he had his flint and tinder box and the small signalling lantern with him. Grahame carried no weapons apart from a small knife and he seemed completely confident. The boat was close to the beach but at a word from Merriman it slowed while Grahame studied the land through a night glass. The image was upside down, but he could see all he needed and pointed to starboard to a small oddly shaped headland. The boat beached gently in a small inlet, they shook hands, and then a sturdy sailor carried Grahame ashore to keep his feet dry. Wet feet and shoes would look very suspicious if he was caught by a patrol.

Chapter Eight

Martinique. More exercises for the crew

All the following day Merriman kept the ship out of sight of land. Too worried to sit still for long, he spent the next quarter of an hour devising new exercises to keep the men occupied. Of course, all the usual routine work was being done when he went up on deck, but he decided to set the men to work on his latest idea. Mr Andrews was Officer of the Watch so Merriman strolled across to him and said quietly, "David, a new exercise. I want each of the two for'ard guns changed over to the other side at once. You stay here and let Mr Gorman take charge with Mr Shrigley."

Andrews gaped for a brief moment, surprised at the unusual order but almost instantly began shouting orders to the petty officers. The crews of the two guns Merriman had selected raced to their places. Merriman ostentatiously looked at his timepiece to see how fast the exercise would take and then stood by the taffrail with his back to the activity. Shouts and rumblings of gun carriage wheels over the deck told of the feverish activity on the gun deck. Eventually a panting and sweating man appeared on the quarter deck to report, knuckling his forehead as he said, "Mr Gorman's compliments, sir, it's done."

"Good, tell Mr Gorman I am coming." The man fled and Merriman slowly walked along the gun deck and made his way for'ard followed by Andrews. The guns had been changed over but Merriman's keen eye spotted a rammer not in its correct place and one of the ropes untidily coiled. "That took you men over twenty minutes," he said, "and it's not finished, look at that rope and the rammer isn't where it should be." He turned to Andrews and Laing who was off watch but who had been awakened by the noise. "Gentlemen, I know I took you all by surprise, but I want it done quicker next time. Dismiss the hands."

He retired to his cabin well satisfied. He waited for the noise and bustle to subside then went on deck again to see his officers discussing the results. "Gentlemen," he said, "I want the same thing done again, the number three guns this time and NOW."

Once again the noise and bustle broke out, orders shouted while he stood there studying his timepiece. This time he was pleased to see that the men had managed to knock two minutes off the previous time and he wondered why he hadn't thought of it before.

That it wasn't an easy operation he knew, the guns had to be secured all the time with chocks behind the wheels and ropes to prevent them taking charge and rolling round like wild beasts weighing several tons, capable of severely injuring or killing men. This was a calm day with the ship hardly rolling but it would be a different matter in rough weather. Merriman called his officers together to give him their comments about the way the work was done.

"Now then, gentlemen, what ideas do you have for an improvement in the time and safety of the men?"

"A difficult task, sir, not one often done," said Andrews, "but I have been watching and I think that with a bit more practice and one or two changes in the order things are done we can do better."

"I'm glad to hear it, David. You and Mr Oakley will take charge next time. The two guns third from aft will be the next and I'll give you ten minutes to organise the crews and tell them your ideas before I give the order."

By now a spirit of competition had infected the gun crews and all those not on lookout duty or involved with actually sailing the ship crowded onto any place they could to see what was going on. Merriman watched while Andrews gathered the gun crews round him to tell them what he wanted. He waited the promised ten minutes then shouted, "Mr Andrews, NOW."

The usual activity started again and at the end of it he was pleased to see nearly another three minutes knocked off the time.

"Better, gentlemen, but I think it could still be improved. I want all of you with the gun captains to put your ideas together. When you have decided, each gun crew will have to be trained accordingly and we'll try again tomorrow. Now dismiss the men back to their normal duties."

Later, Merriman stood at the taffrail staring unseeingly out to sea. It was a lovely sight, the sun was setting in the west with its usual blaze of colours, but it was still hot. Nevertheless, he shivered, his gloomy thoughts casting their shadow over his mind. *What do I do if Grahame never comes back to be picked up, maybe the French will catch him? The best thing would be to go directly to Antigua and report to the Admiral there. No, I can't do that, without Grahame my orders will have no weight and I'll probably find the ship on convoy duty, blast it.*

He wrestled with the problem for a long time with everybody careful not to disturb him. Grahame had said two or three days so all he could do was to close with the shore each night and hope to see Grahame's arranged signal. Gloomily, he went down to his cabin not really seeing the activity going on round him as Mr Cuthbert ordered sail changes to suit a backing wind. He slept badly and all the following day he kept the hands busy with the gun-changing exercise he had devised. The times were improving but still not up to the standard he wanted.

The second night he sent Lieutenant Gorman off with the boat to look for Grahame's signal, but no signal was seen and so another boring day followed as did the third and last day. The men were kept busy with another exercise Merriman had devised involving turning each gun round in a circle before running it back into place. The men seemed to enjoy the unusual work, a change from their usual tasks although the officers and the bos'n and his mates kept a sure eye on the ship in case any unexpected work had to be done.

The third night Merriman felt compelled to go in the boat with Lieutenant Gorman and to go ashore if necessary to find Grahame. They anchored just offshore to wait. The hours passed slowly, and dawn was beginning to colour the sky when they heard shots and Jackson, who had been put ashore as a guard, called quietly, "Somebody coming, sir, only one or two of 'em."

Sure enough it was Grahame, struggling to support another man.

"Into the boat, all of you," said a very relieved Merriman. "Give way together you men. Back to the ship, Mr Gorman."

On board *Aphrodite* an exhausted Grahame told Merriman that the other man was his uncle. "Will you find a place for him and have Mr McBride take a look at him, James? He's an old man but he has done well. I'll tell you everything tomorrow. Now I need a brandy and a good sleep but please get the ship far out to sea and as fast as possible. Some soldiers saw us, but I managed to persuade them that I was only taking my drunken uncle home. I thought they believed me, but I couldn't be certain and after a short hesitation then they came after us."

Chapter Nine

Martinique. Results of Spying

The next morning a rested Grahame joined Merriman on the quarterdeck closely followed by Doctor McBride. "Ah Doctor, how is my uncle this morning?" asked Grahame.

"Tolerably well, sir. He fell asleep as soon as I put him into a hammock last night in the gunroom, he was totally exhausted. He woke about an hour ago and I examined him thoroughly, but he seems healthy enough for his age. He is asleep again now."

"Thank you, Doctor, let us know if there is any change," said Merriman. "Now then, sir, let us retire to my cabin and tell me about your adventures ashore."

Once below and furnished with coffee by the attentive Peters, Grahame began, "It was very worthwhile, James. I found my uncle's plantation easily, but it was very much reduced in size and is little more than a farm now. There had been a slave rebellion earlier this year and most of my uncle's slaves left him and never came back. The French crushed the rebellion and hanged the ringleader with some others, and we suspect my uncle's slaves were probably killed by the French."

He sipped at his coffee whilst he marshalled his thoughts. "Without slaves the plantation could not continue, in fact it had begun to fail after the French took over the island. He couldn't afford to buy more slaves, so his holding was reduced to only a small farm, with three cows and a vegetable garden. The French left him alone, but the upset was too much for my aunt Rachael and she died last year."

"Indeed, I'm sorry for them, but tell me, why did you bring him back with you?"

"Be patient a little longer, James, I have told you the worst and now for the best part. Uncle Edward had lost everything most dear to him, but he managed to eke out a living by going into Fort Royal with cheese and milk from his few cows. He also grew vegetables to sell in the market. This allowed him to hear what the French forces were doing. After the market closed, he would go into a tavern on the quayside and sit quietly in a corner with a meal and a drink, listening to the drunken boasting of the French soldiers and sailors. He heard a lot which will be useful to our commanders."

Another sip of coffee and he continued, "We haven't spoken about it, James, but I'm certain you will have realised that our people must try to take these three islands, St Lucia, Martinique and Guadeloupe from the French. The information my uncle has given me will be invaluable. He wrote nothing down but kept it all in his head and he told me that the French have food but are desperately short of supplies of powder and shot. There are three men of war in the harbour but some of the captains have refused to put to sea without some major repairs to their ships, many of which are rotten with shipworm and disease has cut down the number of sailors. The harbour is short of canvas and rope and many other essentials."

He paused as they heard a knock on the cabin door which opened to reveal McBride and his new patient.

Merriman said, "I'm pleased to see you, sir, I trust you have quite recovered now under the care of our good Doctor?"

"Yes, indeed I have, Captain," replied Edward Grahame. "Thanks to my nephew Laurence and the good Doctor I feel quite rested and glad to be away from the damned French."

"Your nephew has told me much about conditions in Martinique. Please sit down and listen as he continues. Add anything you think he has missed. Please continue, sir," Merriman said turning to Grahame.

"Thank you, James, Uncle Edward has mentioned that there are several privateer ships closer in and they are also in need of refurbishment. Of course, our naval blockade of French ports and our ceaseless patrols here will I hope, stop any supplies from reaching Fort Royal."

"The soldiers, Laurence, have you mentioned the forts and the soldiers?" asked the older Grahame.

"I'm just coming to that, Uncle, I haven't forgotten. So about the soldiers, James, it seems that there were no more than six thousand of them scattered round the island in small forts and batteries but the bulk of them in Fort Bourbon and Fort Royal which defend the harbour. Of that six thousand, many have died, and others are incapacitated by fever. I think that is all, James."

"One other important point, Captain," said Grahame's uncle. "Drink. Many of the soldiers drink too much of the local brew of rum which makes them useless for duty in the mornings. Their officers issue warnings and harsh punishments but they can't stop it."

"Thank you, sir, you have much useful information which we should take to Antigua as swiftly as we can to where I imagine preparations for invasion may be taking place. I would be pleased if you used my sleeping quarters and this cabin during your stay aboard, but for now I must ask you to leave as this space is too small for everyone. I must have all my officers here to tell them what we now know and then I shall tell them what we are going to do."

"Thank you, Captain, but I do not want to inconvenience you and I am quite used to sleeping in a hammock so I must decline your kind offer."

Dawn of the next day found *Aphrodite* with a good wind behind her scudding through the channel between St Lucia and Martinique, under all plain sail. Rounding the southern corner of the island, Point De Salines, they picked up a strong northerly current which added to the ship's speed through the water as the Master, busy with the log line, happily reported. He turned to the two young Midshipmen Shrigley and Oakley. "Now young gentlemen, it's time for your lessons and never mind grumbling. You have to learn if you are to progress further in the navy."

Merriman had ordered the Master to set a course passing as near to the coast as safety demanded so that any of the forts or even new forts could be seen. "From what we have learned, Mr Cuthbert, I don't believe we shall meet any French ships but better to be safe than sorry. Mr Laing, pass the word 'beat to quarters' if you will, but don't run the guns out yet," ordered Merriman.

The ship steered a course to pass between the coast and Diamond Rock, a tall, stiffly upright finger of rock dominating the channel. Merriman, standing aside from all the activity, studied the rock as the ship approached it. He spoke to the First Lieutenant standing close by, "Colin, can you imagine the effect on any French convoys if a pair of twenty five pounders could be swayed up there?"

"Indeed yes, sir, they could stop French convoys coming this way to Fort Royal. They would have to go round to seaward and Mr Cuthbert told me that wind and current could carry them past the port there. Possibly somebody will do it."

Passing Fort Royal Bay, Merriman ordered the *Aphrodite* in closer to see if there were any more ships there than Mr Grahame had told them, but all seemed the same as he had said. As they passed the northerly headland protecting the bay, there came a shout from aloft, "Deck there, sail to larboard. A small cutter, sir, making in our direction."

Merriman snatched a telescope from the rack and studied it carefully before he heard another hail from the man aloft, "Deck there, another ship, sir."

Merriman called to the midshipman, "Mr Shrigley, aloft with you and take a glass, tell me what you see."

Shrigley scampered aloft up to the foremast crosstrees. "A cutter, sir, with a frigate after it. The frigate is one of ours, sir, I can see her colours."

"Come down, Mr Shrigley. Mr Cuthbert, set a course to intercept that cutter if you please, and I'll have the colours shown."

"Aye-aye, Sir," responded the Master.

The wheel was put over and the sails adjusted until the ship was on the new course. The cutter immediately swung away to try and escape but fast though it was, the *Aphrodite* was faster, closing fast.

"A shot across her bows, Mr Laing."

"Aye-aye Sir," replied Laing, shouting orders.

One of the already loaded twelve pounder bow chasers fired and the splash ahead of the cutter was enough. The boat swung up into the wind and dropped her sails. *Aphrodite* hove to, presenting her full broadside to the cutter.

The following frigate was soon up with them and hove to, a string of flags raised. "Captain to come aboard, Sir," piped young Shrigley.

Merriman's boat was quickly in the water leaving Merriman barely enough time to change his uniform and fasten his sword belt before climbing down into it. His big cox'n Owen was at the tiller, roaring orders to the seamen, "Row you buggers, pull like yer lives depend on it or I'll sort you out later."

Owen brought the boat smartly round the stern which displayed the ship's name, *Argonaut,* before bringing it alongside the frigate. Merriman climbed aboard to the usual ceremony of whistles and saluting marines. A lieutenant met him and introduced himself. "I'm the First Lieutenant, Howard by name. Welcome aboard, sir, Captain Wykeham is waiting below."

Captain Wykeham was standing by his desk as Merriman was introduced. "Captain Merriman, who are you and what are your orders? Your ship and number do not appear in my signal book."

"No, sir, news won't have reached here yet, I was only given command of my ship in December and she is absolutely new. As to why I am here, sir, my documents will explain."

Wykeham's eyebrows shot up when he saw the Admiralty orders and the letter signed by none other than Mr Pitt. "That is all very clear, Mr Merriman, and I won't enquire into your activities, must be important for Mr Pitt to be involved. Would you like a drink?" Before Merriman could reply he shouted, "Jones, wine here at once."

Jones must have been expecting the call and waiting just outside the door. He entered almost before his Captain had finished speaking, carrying a silver tray with a bottle of claret and two glasses on it which he proceeded to fill.

Settled behind his desk with a full glass in his hand, Wykeham seemed to relax. "Tell me about your ship, sir, I could see that she is fast, probably faster than my ship. I was barely able to keep up with that cutter, but of course *Argonaut* is heavy with weed, needs a good scraping, you know. In fact until you appeared I was doubtful I would catch her."

They were immersed in technical details of the *Aphrodite* when there was a knock on the door and the marine sentry's voice saying, "First Lieutenant, sir."

Lieutenant Howard entered with another Lieutenant introduced to Merriman as Devlin who made his report to the captain. "I boarded the cutter as ordered, sir, she has a cargo of rope and canvas and other ship's tackle. The captain told me, after a little persuasion, that he was hoping to get into Fort Royal and said he could have done if the sloop hadn't interfered."

"Thank you, Mr Devlin, I'll put you in as prizemaster so pick some reliable men to go with you and you can take her to Antigua. I'm sure the Admiral will want to buy her in, always wants more ships as messengers and for small tasks. A little bit of prize money for us all, what! Captain Merriman, perhaps you would escort the prize to Antigua, don't want to lose it to a privateer, do we? Oh yes, Mr Devlin, put the Frenchies ashore after dark somewhere along the coast, we don't need them."

Chapter Ten

Antigua, Britain's Base in the Leeward Islands

English Harbour in Antigua was the navy's most important base in the Caribbean, heavily fortified, on the southeast coast well sheltered from violent storms, and also protected by a coral reef. Not a large island, being only some one hundred or more square miles, yet it was the gateway to the Caribbean and had the only major dockyard in the region able to carry out repairs on naval vessels.

Sugar was the main crop, cultivated by thousands of slaves controlled by only some three thousand white people. An abortive rebellion had occurred some years previously with the leaders executed. The main difficulty with Antigua was the almost complete lack of rivers, meaning little water which, like wood had to be brought from elsewhere. Some rain was caught in catchments and diverted into cisterns but not nearly enough for the inhabitants' needs.

Aphrodite sailed past Fort Berkley on its headland, into the harbour under a gentle breeze, which did little to blow away the stench of the filthy water. Three large warships plus frigates, sloops and many other vessels were lying at anchor and all the men, some three or four thousand, each used the heads daily for their easement with everything falling into the sea. With no rivers entering the harbour to flush away the accumulating sewage from the ships, no wonder there was a stench. One of the biggest ships was presumably the Admiral's flagship but no Admiral's flag was flying. There was no sign of life on some trading vessels at anchor nearby and one small brig which was heading outward as *Aphrodite* approached. They passed a large sandy beach to starboard with some men digging graves for two canvas-wrapped bodies.

After making the necessary formal gun salutes to the Port Admiral's flag flying over a large building ashore and anchoring in the place indicated by the Harbourmaster's boat, Merriman was vastly relieved. Every detail of sail handling and anchoring had been done immaculately, thanks to the crew's continuous practice. He knew that many telescopes would be trained on every aspect of his ship. His gig was in the water as soon as the ship stopped, with its crew urged on by curses from Merriman's cox'n Owen who would stand for no slackness in the captain's boat.

"Signal from Flag, sir," squeaked little Shrigley, the signals midshipman. "Captain to report to Flag, immediately."

Merriman and Grahame had expected the signal and both climbed down into the boat with Merriman in his best uniform, going last as tradition demanded. The crew pulled lustily and very soon the boat was alongside a timber wharf where a young but sunburnt Lieutenant waited for them. "Captain, Sir, I have orders to take you to the Admiral at once, but I don't know if this other gentleman is to be included."

"He is with me, Lieutenant, so lead on."

The Admiral's offices were almost new and the man himself, Sir William Howarth, was a slim gentleman with a severely sunburnt nose who welcomed them warmly. Shaking Merriman by the hand he commented, "Smart crew you must have there, Captain, we were all watching. I've never seen better ship and sail handling. I am looking forward to having your ship under my command, sir. Now then who is this gentleman with you?"

"May I introduce Mr Grahame, Sir William, a representative of the Government and Treasury, here on urgent business."

"You are welcome, sir. Please sit down, gentlemen. Will you have some refreshment, tea, wine, or rum?" said the Admiral calling for his subordinate.

When settled, each with his preferred drink brought in by an obsequious steward, Merriman began saying, "I have here dispatches for you, sir," as he passed them over. "And there are some bags of mail aboard to be brought ashore. This must be a short visit, a courtesy call really. And as to why we *are* here, sir, I will let Mr Grahame inform you."

The Admiral was beginning to go red in the face at the intimation that he would not have *Aphrodite* under his command, until Merriman passed over his orders from the Admiralty and the letter signed by no less a person than the First Minister Mr Pitt requesting all persons in authority to help in any way needed.

As he read all the documents the Admiral calmed down, looked at them both and exclaimed, "All this is quite clear, gentlemen. I regret that I am not to have you under my command, Mr Merriman, I could always use more ships with the demands made by patrols and convoy escorts. However, it is obvious that your task is just as important. Is there anything I can do to help?"

Grahame coughed to clear his throat and began. "You must know, Admiral, that we have an intelligence service as do the French. Controlled by our Treasury, we have or did have agents all over the Caribbean trying to discover what our enemies are up to. It is my purpose to attempt to contact them all to see what they may have found out or even to find out if they are still alive. We know that the French have their agents over here trying to foment trouble between the slaves and their owners, with their ideals of freedom and equality for slaves. Notably the most recent uprising in San Domingue is a case in point. But those agents will work to the same end in all islands, French, Spanish and of course our own possessions. We must do all we can to stop them. That is why I am here, sir, and Captain Merriman and his ship are to be under my command." He passed over his letter of authority from the Treasury.

"Very well, gentlemen, obviously your mission must be important, now will you tell me what I can do to help?"

"Thank you, sir," said Merriman, "we have need of nothing except some fresh water and a supply of citrus fruit. Mr Grahame will visit a few people here and can also arrange for the fruit. I should mention that it would be as well if word of our duties does not leak out, the French will have agents here too, in fact I met Captain Gordon and his convoy three days ago and he told me that his sailing plan was discussed here just before he sailed. But they were intercepted by privateers well out of sight of land so he thinks you might have a spy here." Merriman went on to describe the action and his good fortune to arrive as it was attacked.

"A spy here in my offices? I suppose that is possible, but I have no idea who it could be, one of the servants maybe. I will certainly look into it. The biggest problem I have is the shortage of able-bodied troops here. These tropical diseases, yellow fever and dysentery kill them off like flies. Another reason is rum, the first distillation from sugar is lethal and kills as many as disease does. The men are so crowded together that disease spreads like wildfire. Things have improved since Colonel Shawcross arrived to take command, he has had the troops spread out more and under canvas, but deaths still occur regularly, and more troops are expected here soon which could make matters worse." He shrugged. "But that is *my* problem, gentlemen, and so far as the activities of privateers are concerned, I can tell you that there has been a suspicious lull in their depredations. They sail from American ports and other islands such as Martinique and Guadeloupe and are either French or American but many of them are no better than pirates. They are the worst and seem to delight in killing innocent seafarers, although some of the privateers are no better regardless of their Letters of Marque."

He continued, "Soon we shall be assembling a large convoy of merchant ships bound for England which will have to be protected. Perhaps they are hoping to make a combined attack on that. They are an ever-present threat and with so few warships under my command I am at my wits' end to keep a naval presence in all the places we should be. Of course, I am under pressure from the owners of those ships to provide as strong a force of my ships as possible to protect them. So, you can see why I had hoped to have your ship available."

Merriman nodded his understanding of the situation.

"Now, you ask for citrus fruit, eh! Captain, are you one of those who think it will prevent scurvy?"

"Indeed I am, sir," replied Merriman. "I am convinced of it and I believe the Admiralty has come round to that way of thinking. You will probably receive orders to that effect, maybe in these new dispatches and they may also inform you that we are again at war with France."

As they walked back to the quayside, Grahame commented, "Well that went better than expected, the Admiral proved to be no problem after all. Anyway, I must visit one of my people here, a merchant by the name of Jonah Cornwall, to see what he knows. He will arrange the supply of fruit, from a yellow fever free area, I hope. So, James, you can go back to the ship and wait for me to appear back on the quay with the fruit when you can send a boat for me. I would be grateful if you could send one of your men with me, in case I need to send a message back to you."

As soon as he returned to the ship, Grahame immediately called Merriman below for a conference and began, "James, it seems to be worse than I thought. England has only Jamaica left in the Greater Antilles. France and Spain have most of the rest including Hispaniola, Puerto Rico, and Cuba. In the Lesser Antilles, we have only scattered possessions: Antigua, where we are now, and Barbados are the most important. There are smaller islands under our control but none of that much importance. Both France and Spain have the surrounding islands - Guadeloupe, St Lucia, and Martinique being the biggest. As you know our fleet and squadrons are stretched to the limit patrolling all the Windward Islands and up into the Leeward Islands."

Here he paused for a sip of orange juice and then continued, "The main problem all over the Indies is that there is a bigger population of African slaves than there is of white managers, overseers and owners of the plantations, and it is those slaves who are in revolt. The result is that many white people fear for their lives, and many have fled or been killed. Production of sugar, tobacco and other exports to England has almost ceased in many places. The Government and the Navy are under increasing pressure from rich and titled owners to do something about it. Of course, we know that French revolutionaries are behind most of the slave revolts with their message of freedom and equality for all. Mr Cornwall has gathered news of many places, but I think we had better start our investigations here and then wherever our information will direct us."

"It sounds desperate, sir," replied Merriman. "If we are forced out of these places, we have little hope of keeping any control in the area. Antigua has the only good shipyard for repairs and stores available for the fleet."

Both men sat silently for some time. Merriman tugging at his ear, a habit of his when confronted with a problem that needed deep thought. "What details has Mr Cornwall found out here which may give us a start?"

"Not a lot that's definite, I'm afraid. He has a good idea where some of the French may be found, in a particular sailor's bar known as The Harlot's Arms in the worst part of town but he is too well known as a fairly wealthy man to venture down there. He could be robbed or even murdered."

Normally there would have been an invitation from the Admiral or the Governor for Merriman and his officers to join them for dinner, but none was forthcoming, so Grahame and Merriman sat up late discussing what action to take.

Chapter Eleven

Antigua. French spies captured

The ship remained at anchor in English Harbour all the next day whilst the watering and supply barges attended to her needs. Normal shipboard maintenance and life continued with the only excitement being when, after repeated threats to keep away had been ignored, a marine dropped a small cannonball into a persistent trader's boat. The wretched man only just managed to paddle ashore before his craft sank.

Under cover of darkness, one of the smallest ship's boats, rowed by two burly seamen with a petty officer in charge, landed Mr Grahame, Owen and two other seamen, Matthews and Jackson, at a dark and deserted part of the harbour. Grahame was dressed as a seaman, and they all carried weapons of one sort or another. Leaving the boat with orders to wait, they headed towards a street which was lit by light streaming through filthy windows of taverns and looked for the particular bar Grahame had been told about.

Inside, they pushed their way into a dense throng of men, mostly seamen by their dress. Their purpose was to see if they could hear any French being spoken or hear anything which might be useful. But the noise, singing and shouting, and the thick tobacco smoke, made it almost impossible. Having been warned of the dangers of drinking the locally made rum, they all drank some of the indifferent ale and, trying to look as if they belonged there, they looked around them. Nobody was taking the slightest bit of notice of them and not hearing or seeing anything useful they left to try another tavern.

Nothing was heard or seen in several other taverns and so, disappointed, they returned to the ship. Merriman met them as they came aboard but could tell from their shaken heads that the foray ashore had been no good. He called Grahame down to his cabin to hear what had happened.

"Nothing happened, James, nothing whatsoever. It was a waste of time; we must think of something else. I don't think I can face drinking any more of that stuff they call ale," Grahame said sipping at a cup of coffee provided by Peters.

"I have an idea," said Merriman, "but I can't help you with it as I don't speak enough French. The man we captured in the Irish Sea, O'Flynn, is trying to teach me but I am very far from fluent. You do speak the language, sir, perhaps if you go into that tavern again with O'Flynn, just the two of you but with Owen and the rest close by, you might speak a few words in French. Perhaps any Frenchman there will hear you and speak to you. I can think of nothing better, sir."

"It's the best idea so far, James. I'll sleep on it, and we may try it tomorrow night."

In the event Grahame decided to go ahead with the plan and O'Flynn was brought into Merriman's cabin and told what was expected of him and what would befall him if he did anything to betray them.

"Oh no, sir, I won't, you can rely on me, sir. Anyway, I don't want to go back to France, I've nothing to go back there for and I could be executed as a traitor, sir." He was referring to the fact that under the threat of hanging he had revealed details of the French plans in the Irish Sea.

It was decided that Grahame and O'Flynn would go ashore again but besides Owen, Thomas, and Mathews, the boat would take a party of well-armed seamen to remain concealed close at hand in case of trouble.

Chapter Twelve

Antigua. French Spies discovered

Entering the tavern again the following night, Grahame and O'Flynn bought ale and tried to find a quiet corner. They were earlier than the previous night and the place was not so full and noisy as before. Grahame could see his other three men in a group, drinking ale quite separate from him but close enough to help if needed. Some time passed and then O'Flynn began to act as though he was drunk, standing up, swaying, and speaking louder and occasionally lapsing into French. Pretending to be nervous, Grahame assumed a guilty, furtive look and dragged him down into his seat.

Nothing happened for a while; O'Flynn continued to mumble curses in French. Grahame tried to look as though he was quietening the man, but he noted a group of three men at another table who were taking an interest in them. Finally, when O'Flynn climbed to his feet and started shouting again they came over, one put his hand over the man's mouth and the other two grabbed his arms and dragged him outside, motioning for Grahame to follow.

They dragged O'Flynn into a dirty, ill-lit alley behind the tavern and whilst one of the men held him the other two, speaking French, asked Grahame who he was.

"Pierre Peabody I am, just a common man, why do you want to know?"

The man looked him up and down and said, "Never you mind why, you have an English name, yet you speak French but with a funny accent, why is that?"

Grahame could see that O'Flynn was apparently near collapse and the man holding him had let him go but he knew that O'Flynn was only acting, which was confirmed by the surreptitious wink he gave. He also noticed Owen and his other men lounging at the corner, ready for his signal.

"French is my second language after German, that's why, and I speak English as well," replied Grahame. "What do you want with me and me mate? We've done you no 'arm."

"If you really are who you say you are you might be of use to us" replied the man. "Your mate is obviously a native Frenchman judging by his volubility in swearing in French but I'm not too sure about you."

"How can we help you? What would you want us to do?" asked Grahame in his strange French accent.

"Be here tomorrow night and tell nobody about this, nothing, do you understand?" said the man.

Grahame nodded and the three men disappeared into the dark. He looked at O'Flynn who was snoring gently, all part of the act, he supposed. He knew they might be watched so he made a show of hoisting the man to his feet and, half carrying him, made his way back into the tavern where he saw Owen and his two companions in a group by the bar. Owen saw him and made a move towards him, but Grahame gave a very small shake of his head to stop any contact.

Dumping O'Flynn on a seat at a vacant table he made his way to the rudimentary bar where he managed to get himself shoulder to shoulder with Owen and ordered two drinks. Hoping any watcher would think it was idle conversation he told Owen to go but to be back tomorrow night with the large party of seamen and some Marines. He returned to O'Flynn with the drinks and shook him as though waking him. The man was wide awake instantly but looked as though he had just woken. Grahame told him what had transpired and after a few more drinks they left to look for somewhere they could sleep for the night.

Chapter Thirteen

High Winds, Deserters and French Spies

Meanwhile, back on the ship, Merriman was desperately worried. Would Grahame learn anything of interest? Would the men return safely? He paced up and down the quarterdeck tugging at his ear and with such a scowl on his face that the duty watch made sure to keep safely to the other side of the deck and in the shadows. Owen had reported what had happened and that he had been told to be there the next night with the extra men but could tell him little more.

Question after question passed through his mind. Was Grahame's agent, Mr Cornwall, an honest man? Had he betrayed Grahame to the French and American privateers? What should he do if Grahame did not return? Exhausted, Merriman stumbled down to his cabin, threw off his coat and fell onto his cot to fall asleep instantly.

He awoke to the usual shipboard noises and the smell of coffee. He was astounded to find that the sunlight was streaming in through the stern windows and to find his man Peters hovering about with a pot of freshly brewed coffee and a cup on a tray.

Merriman struggled to his feet, gave a prodigious yawn, stretched, and sniffed the air. "By God, Peters, that smells good, it should wake me up properly. What have you got for my breakfast?" he said, draining the first cup and holding it out for more.

"Your favourite, sir, some pork fried with breadcrumbs and onions, and some fresh butter on a ship's biscuit, sir."

The coffee indeed worked wonders and Merriman felt ready for the day. "Right, Peters, I'll have my breakfast right away and then you can shave me and I'll change into fresh clothes."

After a shave and in fresh clothes, Merriman stepped out onto the quarter deck feeling like a new man and with his mind made up as to what he should do. Every man immediately tried to look as busy as possible. Lieutenant Laing, who was the officer of the watch crossed towards him.

"Good morning, sir, I trust you have had a good night."

"Excellent, thank you. I didn't think I would, but I slept like a log." Merriman coughed deliberately, annoyed with himself for unbending so far as to discuss his sleeping arrangements with a junior officer, even his first Lieutenant. He looked across the harbour, then up at the sky, sniffed the air and said, "Mr Laing, I think we shall have some bad weather soon. I don't like the look of that line of dark clouds to the east. Pass the word for the Master, if you please."

"You sent for me, sir?" said Mr Cuthbert when he arrived on deck.

"Yes I did. What do you make of that dark line of cloud out there to the east?"

The master took only a moment to make up his mind. "We're in for a blow, sir, a gale and a bad one if I'm any judge. I've seen it before when I was here some years ago. The ship will be safe enough where it is, but I think we should check all the lashings on everything that's tied down. See the other ships, sir, they are doing it."

It was so, men could be seen laying out on the yards checking the sail ties and men in boats were rowing out to lay extra anchors.

"Thank you, Mr Cuthbert. Mr Laing, you will see to it that all that is needed is done. We'll have all hands on deck."

"Aye-Aye, sir." Laing spun round and started shouting orders. At once men boiled up from below with Laing giving orders to all Officers and Petty Officers who in turn bellowed orders to the crew. Lashings on all the guns were reinforced, anything moveable taken below and men were aloft checking everything. The boats were hastily brought on board and secured with extra lashings. The galley fire was extinguished, and hatch covers securely fastened.

Merriman watched everything with his eagle eye which missed nothing. The noise and bustle died away as the first Lieutenant reported all had been done. "Very good, Mr Laing, as you can see, the gale is almost upon us."

Indeed, the bank of dark clouds was nearing rapidly, as the sun disappeared behind the flying clouds which preceded it. A powerful wind had risen and the black clouds were soon overhead releasing a torrent of rainwater which instantly soaked everyone on deck who had not had a chance to find cover. Even in the harbour, which was very well sheltered, the ships were pounded by the wind and rain.

Merriman had fled down to his cabin to change from his uniform into an old one and was back on deck, dressed in tarpaulins and clutching grimly to the quarter deck rail as he tried to see if anything was amiss, but all was well. He was conscious of Midshipman Shrigley grimly holding on to the pinrail round the base of the mizzen mast. After only a few hours the rain ceased, and the sun came out again. Shrigley shook himself like a wet dog and ventured to speak. "Have you been out here before, sir and is it always like this?"

"Indeed I have, young man. I was a midshipman like you, aboard Admiral Rodney's flagship *Formidable* at the Battle of the Saintes in the Dominica channel between Dominica and Guadeloupe. Seventeen eighty two that was, and we roundly trounced the French fleet. As for the weather, we take what comes tho' it is always warmer than the Channel. Now be off with you and dry yourself off."

Shrigley fled below, secretly marvelling that his otherwise strict captain had unbent enough to tell him about being a midshipman at the Saintes. What a tale he would have to tell his fellow midshipman Oakley.

The temperature rose quickly, and steam began to rise from all over the deck and upper works which were soon dry as once again the heat became close to unbearable. Merriman almost envied the seamen working stripped to the waist; his shirt was sodden with sweat but all he could do was unfasten it and try to find some shade as his cabin was like an oven.

The day passed slowly and then night fell as rapidly as usual and the cutter with Owen and the other seamen and marines with their sergeant aboard left the ship with the Second Lieutenant, David Andrews snarling at them to stop chattering and keep silent. Merriman paced the deck in a fever of worry whilst trying desperately not to let his officers see his agitation.

He tried to fill his mind with thoughts of home, but he knew that he would hear nothing for many weeks until the Naval post caught up with them, if it ever did. It was nearly dawn before the lookout on the larboard quarter called to report a boat approaching and Laing called the duty watch of marines to the entry port in case of trouble. It was the cutter with what seemed to be filled with more men than it had when it left the ship.

Mr Grahame climbed wearily aboard followed by the seamen, some sporting grubby bandages. In the middle of them was a group of four men with the abject appearance of prisoners. The marines took charge of them and took them below.

"Watch them carefully, they are a mixture of French, Spanish and some English deserters. Put them in irons," said Grahame to the marine Lieutenant. "And the body in the boat will have to be dealt with."

He followed Merriman down to his cabin where he almost fell into a chair he was so exhausted. Peters, Merriman's servant, appeared out of his hidey-hole and produced a jug of hot coffee.

"My God!" said Grahame after finishing his first cupful in one great draught and holding it out for more. Merriman could hardly wait to hear how the night's events had unfolded and sat down then stood up again and fiddled with things on his desk until Grahame said, "Do sit down, James, I'll tell you everything when I've finished this coffee. Is there any more, Peters?"

"I'll make some more, sir, right away," said the man and he disappeared with the empty jug.

"Now then, James, it was a most successful night. All happened exactly as we hoped. We waited in The Harlot's Arms, that is the inn, James, not a woman, until the same three men came in and ordered O'Flynn and myself to follow them. They took us to a ramshackle building with a lantern over the door and pushed us inside. I saw Jackson following us in the shadows and was able to signal him by taking off my hat and scratching my head as arranged. Did you know, James, that man used to be a poacher, moved in the darkness like a cat. I only saw him because I was looking for him. Anyway, inside the only room there were four other men waiting for us, talking in French and I heard one say something like, "It's all going our way in Jamaica," before they stopped talking and began to question us. We told them the same as we had told them the other night and managed to spin it out until there was a pounding on the door and a voice shouting, "Open in the name of the King."

"Panic followed, some wanted to fight and two tried to get out of a window at the back but were pushed back at the point of bayonets. Then the door crashed open and young Andrews was shouting for us to surrender. The ones who wanted to fight did so furiously but were quickly killed and we took the rest prisoner. Unfortunately one of your men was killed. We brought him back with us but left the others there for their friends to find. I think a bit of forceful questioning of the prisoners will give us some more information, James."

Merriman grinned at Grahame. "Excellent, sir, the plan worked but I must confess that I was very worried about it. Now here's Peters hovering around with some more coffee so I suggest you have some more and then find your way to your cabin, you look as though you can't keep your eyes open."

Not having slept all night, Merriman followed suit, but not before he was sure the injured had been taken care of and all the shore party given a tot of grog. The dead sailor was in the orlop being prepared for a sea burial the next day. Merriman fell asleep well satisfied with the results of the plan.

Chapter Fourteen

Interrogation of Prisoners

Merriman did not sleep for long; he was awakened by shouting and thumping on the quarterdeck above his head. As he groggily called for Peters, the cabin door was flung open by an agitated Owen - his cox'n – who said, "Mr Laing's respects, sir. He apologises for disturbing you but needs you on deck urgently."

"Very well, Owen, I shall be there directly."

Apart from his uniform coat Merriman had not taken his clothes off to sleep and it only took a moment to find his shoes then comb his fingers through his hair before he climbed up on deck. There he was greeted by the sight of a group of men standing round a body and exclaimed, "What's all this then, Mr Laing? Why is that man dead?"

"Sir, he is one of the four prisoners, one of the deserters, I think. He was being questioned by Mr St James when he pulled a knife from his trouser leg and made a bolt for it. He stabbed a marine, sir, fortunately not seriously, and got up on deck before another marine followed and skewered him with his bayonet."

"Damn it man, was he not searched for weapons after his capture, and were they not in irons?"

Laing gestured to a distraught Andrews who had been in charge of the prisoners. "Yes, sir, I did search them but never thought to look in his lower trouser leg. He is one of the English deserters, sir, and would have known that he would be hanged for it so made a last desperate attempt to escape. We took his chains off when we brought him up for questioning. I'm sorry, sir."

"A pity, now we shall never know what he might have told us." Merriman looked at a white-faced marine with a bloodied bayonet. "What have you to say about this and what is your name?"

The man dragged himself up to attention, "Sir, Stokes, sir, an' I was one o' the two guards while Mr St James was questioning 'im. I don't know where 'e got the knife from, sir, but 'e stabbed me mate an' climbed up t'companion way. I followed 'im an' caught 'im, 'e was going to jump overboard, sir, so I stopped 'im. I thought I was doing right, sir." The marine looked into space over Merriman's shoulder, his face a mixture of feelings, wondering if he had done right, in awe of facing his captain and worried that he would be punished.

Merriman turned to the marine officer. "Mr St James, I want no action taken against this man, indeed I wish you to make a favourable mention of him in your report." He turned back to the marine and said, "Did you hear that, Stokes? You did well and Mr St James will say so in his report. Now go and clean that bayonet, I don't want any more blood on my deck."

"Yessir, thank you, sir."

As the very relieved marine left the deck Merriman turned to his officers and said harshly, "I want no repeat of this. These prisoners must be kept in irons at all times, do you understand?"

There was a subdued chorus of, "Yessir," and then he went back below to tell Mr Grahame that one of his potential informers was dead.

"If he was a deserter, James, he wouldn't be missed but I don't think he would have been able to tell us much anyway. Being English they would not have trusted him with anything important."

Having dismissed the fate of the mutineer from his mind, Grahame continued, "Now then, we must ensure that none of the other prisoners has the chance to escape, but how we can make them talk without beating them I'm not sure. Beaten and tortured men would be apt to say what they thought we wanted to know but even then one couldn't trust that information completely."

"During the time you were ill ashore under the care of Doctor Simpson, sir, we devised a plan to trick the French prisoners we held into believing that they were to be shot or hanged at the yardarm. Does it seem to you that one of this group is their leader or was he killed?"

"I think the man who first spoke to me in *The Harlot's Arms* the other night is the leader, he is French and when we arrested them, he shouted 'Fight but if you live don't tell the damned English anything.'"

Merriman told Grahame about the previous plan and a slow smile crossed Grahame's face.

"By God, James, it could work, let us try it."

The three prisoners were brought on deck and arranged in a line. Looking up they saw the noosed ropes over their heads. They knew there was no escape, the grim-faced file of marines in front of them made that certain and they could see the ship's sail maker cutting old canvas into squares, just big enough for bodies to be sewn in. Merriman and Grahame faced the terrified men their faces set like stone. Merriman took the lead.

Speaking in English he said, "You know what is going to happen to you, don't you? You are either traitors to England or Frenchmen, my country's enemies. But if one of you will tell us what we want to know he will have a quick death in front of a firing squad instead of being hanged, or maybe he will be pressed into my crew if what he says is true. Mr Grahame…"

Grahame repeated in French and fractured Spanish what Merriman had said. The three trembling men looked at each other before one fell to his knees in front of them, babbling in English, "I'll tell you all I know, sir. Don't kill me, sir, don't kill me please. I can help you." The wretched man broke down into loud sobs, shaking his head and covering his face with his hands.

The man that Grahame thought to be the leader spat at him, and shouted, "Traitor, coward, they'll kill you anyway."

Merriman turned to the marine officer and said, "Mr St James, have some marines take him down to my cabin, the other two can go back below for now."

Down in Merriman's cabin it was still swelteringly hot, in spite of all the windows and the skylight being open. Merriman and Grahame sat behind the desk facing the trembling man who had to be supported by two marines. "Right, fellow, what is your name and how do you come to be mixed up with Frenchmen and privateers?" asked Merriman.

"Plover, sir, Benjamin Plover. Sir, please don't kill me, I can 'elp you if your honour will let me," the terrified man stammered.

Merriman regarded him with a baleful expression on his face. "Benjamin Plover eh, sounds like you are from Devon or maybe Cornwall, which is it?"

"Me Mam's from Devon, sir. I didn't know me father, sir, and I don't think me Mam did either. I earned a living from fishin' but when she died, I joined as crew on a merchant ship out of Plymouth, sir. We was taken by privateers near Bermuda I think it was. We couldn't fight, sir, there was too many of 'em. They killed the captain and mate and took six of us prisoner and made us crew for them. We would be killed if we did anything wrong, sir. Two of me mates tried to escape one night but they were caught and shot. I can tell you some of the places where the privateers 'ide, sir."

"That's as may be, Plover, we shall see," said Merriman in a bored tone before telling the marines to take him down to the gunroom. The other two men, both chained, sat fearfully below guarded by marines who looked ready to kill them on any excuse. They heard the muted sound of a volley of musketry and looked at each other, white faced and shaking. Minutes later they were dragged up on deck where they saw what they assumed was the body of the third man lying face down in the scuppers, his shirt covered in blood. One of the men fainted but the man nearest to the rail - the man that Grahame thought was their leader - managed in spite of his chains to throw himself overboard where the weight of them quickly dragged him down to his death.

"Throw some water over that fellow and bring him below," Merriman told Laing. "We'll see what he will tell us."

When the man was dragged in, Merriman said, "What do you know of the activities of privateers and the French in these islands and who informs them about the movements of the King's ships? Tell me what you can and maybe you will live."

The man looked at the deck. "What's the point, you'll kill me anyway like you did with my mate poor Benjamin. At that point his bladder emptied and he collapsed on the floor.

"You marines, drag him out of here and have somebody bring a mop to clean up this mess." Turning to Grahame, Merriman said, "We'll let him recover and then show him that Plover isn't dead and it was all a trick. Maybe he will be more co-operative next time."

"We must remember, James, I heard one of the men we killed or arrested in the house said something to the effect that 'Things were going their way in Jamaica'. It could be possible that all the French agents and their followers are in some way controlled from one place and one man."

As Merriman suspected, upon his next interrogation, co-operative the man certainly was. He couldn't talk fast enough, revealing what he knew about French agents and others who were trying to foment trouble amongst the slaves. Unfortunately, he didn't know much about other islands than Antigua but enough to tell them about the places other than The Harlot's Arms where conspirators might be found in Antigua.

"I think we should take these two ashore to the Admiral and the Senior Army Commander to interrogate further," said Grahame. "They won't be as lenient as we have been and surely, they will be able to get more out of them. Besides that, they have the men and resources to follow up on anything they discover, and they can also follow up on the news we did manage to get from these two."

"Yes, sir, I agree. Do you wish to stay any longer here in Antigua or are we to move on?"

"Eventually we'll move on, James, but first we must wait and see what the army has learned from the prisoners and what they are going to do. If more foreign agents can be found, then we might learn more."

The following morning, a harassed Flag Lieutenant came aboard with news that Admiral Howarth wished to see them at once. Merriman and Grahame arrived at the Admiral's office to find him in the company a tall, elegant officer dressed in an immaculate red coat with plenty of gold braid, spotless white breeches and black boots polished to a gleaming perfection. He was introduced as Colonel Henry Shawcross, and the officer with him, also immaculately dressed, as Major Heath-Jones.

When they were all settled with refreshment to hand, the Colonel began by thanking Merriman and Grahame for their part in uncovering several groups of French troublemakers.

"Marvellous work, gentlemen. In the short time you have been here you have found and captured the kind of men we have been seeking for a long time. The two prisoners you sent to us have been chattering ceaselessly, helped by my sergeant, a big man who would make a stone talk, and we now have a good idea where we may find more of them. Some stay at two isolated plantations and travel around trying to stir up the slaves with their revolutionary talk and they have a ship anchored in a small inlet in the north of Antigua to pass news and information between the islands."

Grahame nodded his approval and said, "Colonel, we seem to be getting somewhere, and now I must reveal to you the information we have learned about French dispositions in St Lucia and Martinique." He went on to relate what they knew and how they came by the information.

The colonel sat upright with a start of surprise. "Ye gods, this is invaluable information, gentlemen. We must send it to Barbados as fast as possible to Sir Charles Grey who should have arrived there by now. He is to be in command of the new expedition being planned. If you could arrange that, Admiral, I would be vastly obliged. In the meanwhile, we should acquaint Captain Merriman and Mr Grahame with what is happening out here. You will realise that an invasion of Martinique and other islands is being planned under the orders of Sir Charles Grey and the ships gathering in the harbour are all part of it. More are expected with more men from various regiments. There is little we can do here to expedite matters, so I'll tell you what we propose to do here in Antigua."

"Colonel, what parts of your plan are we are to be involved in, if at all?" asked Merriman.

The Admiral broke in, "Colonel, if I may interrupt you, it is for me to tell Captain Merriman what we would like him to do. Gentlemen, the army is ready to start off in the morning, before first light, both infantry and cavalry, to travel as fast as they can to the plantations where we hope these villains might be found. They will catch some, but word of our movements will spread quickly, and we think that others will move northward to where their ship is hidden to make their escape. That is where you come in. You will have seen that most of my small ships have left here, mostly on short, quick and various missions and patrols. They will be back soon but in the meanwhile I wish you to sail rapidly up the west coast to try and find that ship and take it. I am expecting another sloop here shortly, and I will send it up the east side and perhaps between you, you will catch them." He paused for their nods of assent. "I know that you, Mr Merriman, have Admiralty orders to help Mr Grahame with his own duties, indeed the documents you have shown me make that quite clear, but I think that this operation will coincide with your orders. If we do capture a good number, then surely much more information might be learned about the activities of pirates and privateers and rebels in and around these islands. What do you say, gentlemen?"

Merriman turned to Grahame with his eyebrows raised, but before he could speak Grahame said, "I think that is an excellent idea, gentlemen. The ship has been well supplied for several weeks and we need all the information we can get. Can we start at first light, James?"

"I do not see why not, sir; we and the crew will be well pleased to get away from the stink in the harbour."

So, the plan was agreed. As they parted the Colonel wished them luck and said he hoped all would go well.

Chapter Fifteen

Joint Naval and Army Action

First light the next morning found *Aphrodite* moving out of English Harbour and turning north past Shirley Heights fort and signalling station on to pass up as close as close to the shore as prudent navigation demanded. There were numerous small inlets with small local shipping but nothing big enough to be a privateer.

Merriman had already told his officers what their task was and enjoined upon them the necessity of everything being prepared to fight one or maybe two privateers. "There may well be hand to hand work if we find one, so have all the cutlasses and pikes given an extra edge on the grindstone. We acquitted ourselves well in the encounter with the privateers before we reached Barbados, and we must do it again. The Admiral has told me that he intends to send another sloop round the island the other way to try and find our quarry, so between us we should catch something. That is all, gentlemen, I know I can rely on you to a man."

All morning went by without sight of anything warranting further investigation. Merriman was getting increasingly restless, striding up and down the quarter deck with a scowl on his face so that all the people there were at pains to keep out of his way. A significant throat clearing behind him interrupted his thoughts and made him turn with a harsh remark, to find Mr Cuthbert the Master standing there. "What the devil is it now, Master?"

The master was holding a rolled chart and said, "I am sorry to disturb you, sir, but I have been going through some of my old notes and some other notes and new navigation details about the coast given to me by other masters while we were at anchor. I think our best chance of finding any privateers will be when we have passed round the northern tip of the island. Of course, we must look everywhere we can, but if you will look at the chart now, sir, I think you will see what I mean."

"Very well, Master, bring it to my cabin and we'll spread it out."

That was soon done and as they bent over it Mr Cuthbert pointed out certain places. "There are many small places, sir, but the best anchorages can be found in Parham harbour, Guiana Island and Mercers Creek. I had no idea my chart was so much out of date until I transferred all my new information to it."

"Indeed, I think you may be right, Master, those places certainly seem to have more possibilities. As you know, the army is moving up the island to plantations and other places our prisoners revealed to them with the aim of driving as many rebels and privateers before them as they can. In view of that we could expect them to run to wherever their ship is."

Merriman turned and looked out of the cabin windows while he considered what to do whilst the Master waited quietly for his orders. "Right then, Mr Cuthbert, we must head to those places with all speed. Plot the best course for us and then we will be about it."

Ashore, the army had been moving steadily northward up the island along well defined roads and in several groups commanded by either a lieutenant or sergeant. They had captured some men by suddenly surrounding those places they had been told of. True, some men had escaped capture and others who had resisted had been killed, but Colonel Shawcross was well pleased with the results he had so far. He noted that the men not captured had all fled northwards as had been hoped.

The *Aphrodite,* under full sail, rounded the northern coast and approached the first of the bays suggested by the Master, Parham Harbour. This was a wide bay and although they cruised slowly round no ships of any sort were found. They moved on to the next target, Guiana Island which formed the southern side of a long, wide anchorage open to easterly gales but with smaller bays and inlets off it forming more sheltered anchorages. All had to be investigated and Merriman was beginning to have doubts about the possibility of finding anything there, but he kept up his pose of confidence, strolling round the ship and talking to members of his officers and crew.

Back on the quarterdeck he looked at all the officers gathered there and then, pacing up and down, he made up his mind. He turned to the First Lieutenant. "Colin, from Mr Cuthbert's revised chart I think that this is the most likely place to find what we are looking for. I'll have the men on their toes so beat to quarters and take the courses off her. Have the guns loaded with solid shot but not run out, keep the port lids closed."

Standing amidst the sudden noise and bustle, Merriman again doubted if they would find anything, but he reminded himself he must appear confident to all. *Aphrodite* entered the bay under the reduced sail, passing Guiana Island to larboard with extra lookouts aloft viewing every inch of the coast of the island. They had nearly reached the further end of the bay and Merriman was about to order the ship to go about when the boom of a cannon was heard and a spout of water rose just off the larboard side.

"Somebody there doesn't want us any closer," said Merriman. "Did anybody note where that shot came from?"

"Yes, sir, I did, I was looking at the shore and I saw a puff of smoke from among the thin trees just to the left of that small headland, sir," said Oakley, one of the midshipmen.

"Well spotted, Mr Oakley, did anybody else see it? Did you, Mr Cuthbert?"

"Yes, sir, I did and took a bearing on it. We could find it again."

The *Aphrodite* had not yet turned and as they passed the small headland two small ships were revealed at anchor in line astern in the narrow passage between the island and the mainland with a small boat carrying men out to one of them. Musket fire could be heard on the mainland and hardly had they been seen when more cannon fire erupted from the trees.

Most shot either went wide or short but one ball struck the fo'c'sle railing, shattering it and sending a hail of small splinters among the crew there. One man was killed. Merriman was later told that it was one of the pressed men, originally very fat, who had been involved with French agents in England in a plot involving Irish rebels.

"Mr Grahame, I think you and your uncle should go below," said Merriman.

"No, sir, I want to stay on deck to see what we have caught. Anything I can learn about these fellows could be valuable."

"As you insist, sir. Mr Laing," said Merriman formally "have the guns run out. We'll go about and give those gun positions a broadside. Mr Andrews, you have seen where the guns ashore are, so for'ard with you ready to open fire as your guns bear, starboard battery only, and tell Mr Gorman his turn will come."

"Aye-aye, sir," Andrews replied, his face alight at the prospect of action.

Mr Laing bellowed the orders and the ship almost turned on the spot thanks to a keen crew, the weeks and months of training and the continual practice they had grown so used to.

Approaching the small headland again, the site of the gun position revealed itself and Andrews roared out, "As your guns bear – fire."

The blast of shot seemed to cut down most of the trees concealing the cannon, two of which could be seen tumbling through the air.

"Mr St James," ordered Merriman, "as we go about you will take the cutter and half of your marines and investigate ashore. If there are still any usable cannon you will spike them and bring any men you find alive back to the ship."

Under closely reefed topsail and a jib sail *Aphrodite* crept slowly towards where the two small ships were anchored until the man in the fore chains with the lead bellowed, "By the mark five."

"Shoals rapidly here, sir," called Mr Cuthbert from his place by the wheel.

"Very well, Mr Cuthbert, Mr Laing, stop her and anchor here," called Merriman.

Laing shouted the orders, and the topsail was swung into the wind to press against the forward motion of the ship and act as a brake. Once the way was off her the anchor splashed down.

Merriman blessed the forethought which had made him keep the anchor ready for quick use and it had been prepared and lashed to the cathead ever since leaving English Harbour.

"I can see redcoats ashore, sir, on what I suppose we should call the mainland," said Laing, peering intently through his glass.

"Indeed, you can, I see them too," remarked Merriman. "They are pushing a group of men with them, must be the spies and agents they have captured, and I see that more men are trying to go aboard the nearer of those two ships lying ahead of us, so I want to stop them. Have one of the bow chasers put a ball close to the side of the first ship."

That single shot and the waterspout which followed drenched the men in the boat. The implied threat of more stopped them rowing towards their ship and they immediately turned to row back towards the shore where the sight of a line of redcoats with levelled muskets stopped them again.

"Mr St James and his party are coming back, sir, with prisoners I think," said Midshipman Shrigley.

"Very well, Mr Laing, have another ball put into the water on the other side of that ship. I don't want any of those men escaping to the island."

That ball raised another great splash which either killed men in the water or drenched those thinking of jumping in.

The cutter came alongside, and St James and his men climbed aboard with three other men. "The guns are all destroyed, sir," he reported, "and we have only these three prisoners. All the others must have fled into the forest, sir. We couldn't find them, and I judged it wiser not to follow with the few men I had. These three were stunned but otherwise unhurt and gave us no trouble. Only one of my men was slightly wounded."

"Thank you, Lieutenant, you have done well. Now have the prisoners taken below and have all your men ready to go with the party assembled here and board those ships ahead. Use only the force necessary to control them as all of them will have to be questioned. I will go ashore and meet the army fellows."

On stepping ashore accompanied by two seamen - Matthews and Jackson - and leaving his bos'n Owen in charge of the boat's crew, Merriman was met by a sergeant. This man led him to Colonel Shawcross who was sitting down against a tree with his leg stretched out before him, one of his men fussing over a bandage.

"I'm glad to see you, Mr Merriman, I would stand but I got too close to the action and got a musket ball in the leg, damn it." He extended his arm and gingerly shook hands. "You arrived at the right time, sir, we caught some prisoners, and I was wondering how to deal with them. My lads are worn out and if I tried to march the prisoners back to English Harbour I think we would lose more of them."

"I see no difficulty over that, sir, we now have three ships which should be enough to take all your men and the prisoners aboard. Of more concern, sir, is your wound. Has your man dealt with it well enough?"

A bang of cannon fire made Merriman break off and he returned to the beach to see one of the two ships already moving with more sail being set as he watched. A second cannon fired, and the ball bounced like a smooth pebble on a pond and crashed into the stern of the moving vessel but did nothing to slow it down.

"Damn and damn it again," Merriman said as he realised that from where *Aphrodite* was anchored the second ship masked the escaping ship from any more shot. It soon had more sail set and was making swift progress. Merriman knew that there was nothing more that could be done to stop it. It was cutter rigged and must have been of shallow draught to skim over the shallows as it did.

He returned to Colonel Shawcross and said, "I'm sorry, sir, we have only two ships now. My men boarded the first one but before they could reach the second one it sailed." He explained why they could do no more.

"A great pity that, Mr Merriman. I wouldn't be surprised if the leader of all these troublemakers was aboard and we will not catch him now. Damn them all, sir, damn them all."

"Well, sir we have a good many prisoners, both yours and mine, and between us we should be able to extract more information from them." He stopped as he saw Shawcross grimacing with pain and clutching his leg. "Colonel, did your man manage to get the ball out?"

"No, it will have to wait until I can get to a competent surgeon."

"I have a very competent doctor aboard my ship, sir. He is well used to dealing with such injuries. I'll have him brought ashore right away to look at it."

"He will do more than look at it I hope," gasped the soldier with sweat running down his face.

"Jackson, back to the boat and tell Owen to go and fetch Doctor McBride here as fast as possible. Quickly now," ordered Merriman.

A brief, "Aye-aye, sir," and Jackson was sprinting to the boat.

Merriman returned to the colonel to find two junior officers gathered round him looking down helplessly at their commanding officer. "You can't help him, and my own doctor will be here in a few moments. Have you any more seriously wounded here?" he asked.

One officer stepped forward, "I am Captain Blythe, sir. We have several minor injuries, cuts, and bruises and one broken arm but nothing serious, sir, except for the Colonel although we have two dead men. Is your man a good doctor?"

"Indeed, he is Captain, he is the best I have met in all my seagoing life. Your Colonel will be in good hands." He paused a moment, thinking, then asked, "How many of your men and prisoners do you have, Captain? We will have to find space for them all in the two ships for the journey back to your base at English Harbour."

"It would have been three ships if you hadn't let one escape," muttered a Lieutenant. "Bloody carelessness if you ask me."

"Shut your mouth, Lieutenant Orson," snarled Captain Blythe. "You will apologise to this officer, now."

The Lieutenant stalked off after a brief but grudging apology.

"May I also add my apologies, sir. That officer has been a useless soldier ever since he arrived here and a complete nuisance to me."

"Think no more about it, Captain, and if I'm not mistaken I believe Doctor McBride is here."

He was and appeared carrying his bag of instruments together with one of his assistants, a loblolly boy, carrying a larger bag. "Move away, gentlemen, and allow me to do what I was summoned to do," McBride said. He raised the Colonel's leg gently as the assistant slid an old sheet beneath it and then he removed the blood soaked bandage. "I am sorry, sir, but I will have to cut your breeches to get to the wound. You boy, pull off his boot, gently now, you fool," he said as the Colonel groaned in pain.

Swiftly he slit the breeches leg and cut it off completely. He examined the wound, out of which blood was seeping, raised the leg to feel the back of the leg, all the while murmuring as doctors do, "Hmm, aha, thought so, hmmm." Finally he said, "The ball didn't penetrate right through, Colonel, I shall have to probe for it." He turned to the watching men, "Have you got any clean hot water here?"

"Yes, Doctor, the men have a fire going to brew tea of a kind. I'll tell one of them to bring a canteen of freshly boiled water."

The water soon arrived, and McBride gently swabbed the wound with hot water while Shawcross writhed in pain. "Now, if somebody can lift his head a little I will give him something so that he will feel no pain."

"One of Doctor Simpson's magic potions, Doctor?" whispered Merriman as the doctor tipped a small draught of something into his patients' mouth.

"Yes, James, it is, he taught me a lot, as you know. You will see the result in a moment." He dropped some of his instruments into a small bowl, tipped some brandy into it and rinsed them about.

The result of the 'magic potion' was amazing; the colonel stopped writhing and subsided into unconsciousness. "Now then, gentlemen, if one or two of you will hold him down I'll begin. Unconscious though he is he will feel something."

McBride took his instruments out of the bowl, looked regretfully at the brandy before throwing it away and turned back to Shawcross with a long probe in his hand. Inserting it gently into the wound he probed around until he felt resistance then drew it out. With a pair of long forceps, he again probed then pulled them out with the bloody musket ball firmly gripped by the instrument. "Ha, there it is, gentlemen, the subject of all the man's pain."

He dropped the ball into the bowl before again probing with the forceps before pulling out a scrap of blood soaked cloth. Then, rummaging in his bag, he produced a small glass vial and tipped a few drops of a liquid into the wound. The assistant was ready with padding and bandages which McBride deftly used to bind up the wound after he put a stitch or two in to close it up.

"Another of the Doctor's potions Mr McBride?" queried Merriman.

"Yes it is, sir. The Colonel will be alright in good time, but he will need rest with his leg supported. He can't travel overland so I think we shall have to convey him by ship."

"Right you are, Doctor, take him back to the ship and put him in my cot." A makeshift stretcher was made and the injured man was quickly carried aboard with McBride fussing about him all the way.

Merriman turned back to the other men. "Captain Blythe, I was asking you how many prisoners you have and how many of your men will we have to find room for?"

"Ten prisoners, sir, including four Negroes. We should have had more but many men ran before we could catch them. They would have alerted more of the villains ahead of us before the infantry could get there. There are fifty three of our men and two dead men and three horses too, sir, including the Colonel's favourite mare."

"Thank you, Captain, if you could arrange with my officers for all of them to be divided into two groups ready to be taken out to the ships. Then, if your Colonel would agree, I will bury the two dead at sea. We have many prisoners as well so they must be counted in. As for your horses, perhaps we can manage to find space for them on deck. Now I must get back to my ship and make preparations to receive all our new passengers. I will send the boats to pick you all up."

Back on board, welcomed with the usual ceremony beloved by the navy, Merriman was surrounded by his officers with Mr Laing eager to report what had happened whilst he was ashore. "I am sorry one of them got away, sir, our boarding party had only just reached the first of them when the other started away. We could fire only two shots, sir, before she was hidden behind the one we captured."

"I thought that would be the case, Mr Laing. How many prisoners did you take?"

"Twelve, sir, a miserable lot. Three that the marines caught ashore and nine aboard the ship we captured, all of them white men. There are three Negroes as well, probably escaped slaves, sir, but none of them put up a fight. And one of our two shots did hit the stern of the other ship but with what damage I couldn't say, sir."

"Thank you, Colin. There will be more prisoners coming aboard and redcoats too. We can split them between both ships so space must be found for them. There will be some discomfort, but it is not far back to the harbour, so it won't last long. Another thing, we must try and get three horses aboard as well, so have the carpenter build some temporary stalls for them."

An appalled Laing stuttered, "Hor –horses, sir, must we? Think of the mess on your decks, how can we bring them aboard anyway without a jetty?" He broke off as Merriman grinned at him.

"Spoken like a good First Lieutenant, Colin, I know how much you love a clean deck. How will we do it? Well, they can swim out behind a boat after all the men are aboard and then swimmers can get a strop under them. Then they can be hoisted aboard, a straightforward business I think. Now I must go below to see the Doctor's patient for a few minutes."

In his small cabin, Merriman found McBride sitting on a chair looking into the small sleeping space at his patient in the swinging cot. "How is he, Doctor, has he come round yet?"

"Yes, sir, briefly but I assured him all was well, and arrangements were in hand to bring his men and prisoners aboard. He smiled, started to say something but fell asleep. He will recover, sir; he may limp a bit for a while but there should be no lasting damage I am sure."

Back on deck, Merriman found Captain Blythe talking to Lieutenant Andrews, asking what he could do to help.

"Frankly, sir, not a lot. The prisoners will be confined below with our marines on guard and your men put wherever we can find room for them so that they won't get in the way of our men sailing the ship. What you might do, sir, is to see that your men do as they are told by my warrant officers and have one or two of your own officers on the other ship to do the same."

Merriman listened, making no attempt to interfere until Andrews had finished speaking. "I think that is the best plan, Lieutenant. Do you agree, Captain?"

Blythe smiled and said, "We are in your hands, sir, none of my people know anything about ships so they will do as you say if they know what is good for them."

So it was all arranged. A little over half the passengers were brought aboard Merriman's bigger ship together with the horses. That procedure brought a mixture of curses from the seamen doing their best to control the frightened animals and laughter from the men watching until one of the soldiers asked his captain if he could help.

"Used to be a groom before I joined the army, sir. I know a thing or two about the animals, sir."

On being given permission, he removed his jacket and jumped overboard with it. Then he climbed astride one of the struggling horses and draped his jacket over its eyes, whereupon it stopped struggling and was lifted easily onto the deck and put into the temporary stall. The same thing was done with the other two and they were also secured in their stalls.

"All aboard and secure, sir," reported Lieutenant Laing, finally. "The prisoners are below in both ships with our marines guarding them. Most of the soldiers are asleep, worn out with all that marching and running I suppose."

Indeed, Merriman could see most of them were squeezed in between the guns and any other corner they could find.

"Well done, Colin, signal the other ship to get under way and follow us out. Carry on."

Fortunately, the weather was fine with only a strong breeze and his seamen divided between the two ships managed to cope, although Merriman could see some redcoats helping to pull and haul. Once out of the bay, the ships encountered a pronounced swell and soon there were wails of discomfort from the soldiers.

"Not on the deck, not on the deck, you men, overboard if you must, blast you," yelled Laing and soon a line of red coats were lined up along the side where they could find room.

Merriman's servant, Peters, appeared on deck. "The Doctor's compliments, sir, and he asks you to come below. The Colonel is awake and wants to see you."

In his cabin, Merriman had to step over some of the army officers fast asleep on the deck. He found Shawcross wide awake with McBride at his side.

"Ah, Captain Merriman, sir, I am told that all my men and the prisoners are on both ships, and we are on our way back. I can't thank you enough and your good Doctor McBride here is as marvellous as you said. I can't feel anything but slight ache and soreness in my leg."

"That may be so, Colonel, but you must not be tempted to walk on it too soon. I put two small stitches in to close up the wound and they must come out in a few days," said McBride.

There was no deterioration in the weather and after only a few hours they were safely anchored in English Harbour where they saw another sloop with her main topmast missing. The soldiers were ferried ashore with the prisoners to be duly secured in army cells and an empty stone storehouse. The officers waited until last, each wanting to shake Merriman's hand and thank him, all except the unpleasant Lieutenant Orson who stood with his back to them.

Night had fallen by the time they had all left, but the crew worked on by lantern light, cleaning up the rubbish left behind by horses and men, dismantling the stalls and scrubbing the decks. Merriman sent a message to the Admiral by his third Lieutenant, that he would, with the Admiral's permission, report to him in the early morning with a full report on the events of the day.

Chapter Sixteen

Traitors arrive in Jamaica

Jamaica was home to the biggest slave market in the Caribbean, except for those in Louisiana, and had been a British possession since 1655. It was a beautiful island with high mountains in the eastern and northerly parts, covered with dense forest. Sugar and coffee plantations covered much of the level ground and were highly dependent on slave labour, black slaves from Africa brought across in the infamous triangle trade. Eventually and inevitably the slaves soon outnumbered the white owners and overseers who enforced discipline by the use of the whip and other brutal means. Many slaves escaped and were called Maroons. They fled into the mountains where they established their own villages. While the British army tried to suppress them, it was to no avail. The thick forest and mountains hid them far too well.

Kingston was Jamaica's principal town since Port Royal had been destroyed by an earthquake. A little further north one morning, two men found themselves on a deserted wharf well away from any town. The captain of a slave ship had dropped them ashore with a few curses about their being a useless waste of space, thrown them a few coins and their bags and abandoned them. The larger of the two men picked up the precious coins and in the growing light they both sat down to assess which of their belongings had been left to them and to discuss their plans.

Some rumpled clothing and shoes were all they had apart from the few copper and silver coins the captain had thrown. The smaller man spoke first. "Well, the clothes are wearable but badly creased. The money might be enough to get us a room somewhere and our clothes made more presentable. Then a good meal inside us will make us feel better."

That decided upon, they began a long weary trudge to find somewhere to suit their needs.

"My God," said the bigger man, "I can still feel that bloody captain's lash on my back it is so sore, but we're better off now than we were on that stinking ship of death, don't you think?"

The smaller man agreed, "Yes we are at that, but we still have to earn a living somehow. Although anything would be better than throwing the dead, stinking bodies of those slaves overboard and washing down the bilges afterward."

Many weeks ago they had escaped the law in England where they were wanted for murder and treason to the Crown and, after bartering with a ship's captain in Liverpool, they thought that they had managed to arrange passage to the Americas, Boston or New York, on a ship loading trade goods. But the captain was a rogue who had robbed them and forced them to work on the ship which turned out to be a slaver. He had them doing all the dirtiest and most menial jobs aboard.

As they trudged along, the bigger man began to feel more hopeful. "You know, Beadle, it occurs to me that we can both read, write, and do arithmetic. Perhaps we could find work as clerks or something in some trading establishment. What do you think?"

"It's possible, I suppose, but we shall have to make ourselves much more respectable before that. A shave and a bath spring to mind, and disposing of these filthy rags we are wearing."

Eventually they found a river, dragged off the rags and immersed themselves in clean water. "God above, this is good," said the small man, vigorously scratching his long greasy hair and scalp and ducking under repeatedly. He grabbed a clump of grass and began using it as a sponge to clean his body. The bigger man said nothing, being too occupied in doing the same. At last, they emerged, the hot sun soon dried them, and they began to dress in the better clothing.

"You've lost a lot of weight in the last months, haven't you?" said the small man with a grin. "That coat looks as if it was made for a much bigger man."

"All right, all right, you don't look any better," was the retort.

Now feeling better, they continued plodding on until they came to a road, more of a cart track really and sat down hoping they might get a lift on a passing cart.

Eventually one came along, an ancient rickety wagon pulled by two half-starved mules and driven by an aged Negro. They stopped it by the simple expedient of holding the mules' bridles.

"Where are you going, old man? We need a ride," shouted the bigger man.

"To the next village, sir," said the man obsequiously. "I'm taking these barrels to the inn only a mile away from here."

The two men grinned at each other and climbed onto the cart. Arriving at the inn, a shabby rundown sort of a place, they entered to find it was better than its outward appearances suggested. There was only one man behind a crude bar who looked at them suspiciously.

"What do you want here?" he asked. "I don't serve scruffy strangers, especially those who appear to have no money."

The bigger of the two men hastily introduced them, telling the man the story that they had previously agreed upon. "We were on a small coastal vessel going to Kingston. It was attacked by a privateer, ransacked, and sent on its way. We asked the captain to put us ashore before it happened again, which he did but the boat was capsized by a wave. I don't know what happened to the man rowing the boat, we never saw him again. We managed to get ashore, but our baggage was lost, and we seem to have walked miles before we were picked up by that man and his cart. We do have some money, perhaps enough to pay for a bath and a good meal. If someone could try and clean our clothes perhaps we could stay the night and go tomorrow?"

"Your story sounds reasonable but who are you and what is your business in Jamaica?" asked the man.

"Well, sir, I am a lawyer and my name is Jeremiah Robinson. We were hoping to set up a new office in Kingston. This is Beadle, my clerk. We are not asking for charity, sir, but any help you can give us would be appreciated."

"Well show me the colour of your money first and I'll see what I can do."

The landlord seemed satisfied and said, "You both look as though you need a bath, then I can give you a good meal and you can sleep in the barn. My woman will do something with your clothes. Tomorrow will be market day in Kingston and a lot of carts will be going that way so you may get a ride."

The following morning, they woke early. Brushing straw off themselves and putting on the clothing the innkeeper's wife had cleaned they began to feel more optimistic. A sparse breakfast and their thanks to the host and they were on their way in another rickety wagon loaded with bales of straw. Before they left, the innkeeper told them to go to see one Isaac Meyberg in Ship Road in Kingston, who may help them.

Eventually, by means of the old jolting cart they reached Kingston and, after making enquiries, they found themselves outside the premises of Isaac Meyberg. It was a small place cramped between larger buildings, most of them chandlers shops and stores and it was the dirtiest and most unprepossessing of them all. The windows were so filthy that Beadle wondered if anyone could see out of them, while the paintwork was peeling off window frames and the only door. That they were in the right place was confirmed by a dirty and damaged sign over the door proclaiming to passers-by that it was indeed the office of Isaac Meyberg - Lawyer, Actuary and Moneylender. In smaller almost indecipherable letters it announced that he was a Scribe, charging by the hour.

"As we are here we might as well go in, although I'm not hopeful that it will do us any good," said Robinson miserably.

Opening the front door showed a gloomy and filthy passage with two doors on the right hand side. At the end was another door with a light showing round it. They crept forward and Beadle apprehensively knocked whereupon it was flung open by a very large man. 'Fat' would hardly describe him; he was grossly overweight with a huge protuberant belly and several double chins and fingers like sausages.

"Who are you, what do you want?" he snarled, looking them up and down.

"We-we- we were told to come here to see Mr Meyberg," stammered an intimidated Robinson.

"Oh an' 'oo told ye that?" shouted the man.

"I don't know his name, but he runs the old inn out to the west of town. We are looking for work and he suggested we came here. If I'm wrong we can go and not bother you."

"Wait there," said the fat man. He closed the door but reopened it only moments later, ushered them into a surprisingly clean and well-lit office with a huge desk in the middle. A grey haired, wrinkle-faced old man with a long beard sat behind the desk. Flinty grey eyes studied them for several minutes before the man spoke.

"Who are you and what do you think you can do for me you scruffy pair of rogues?"

Robinson launched into their agreed story, but the man gestured for him to be quiet. "I know all that," he said. "My friend at the inn sent a message to me last night. You say you are a lawyer and a clerk, but I repeat, what do you think you can do for me?"

"It is true, I am a lawyer and Mr Beadle is my clerk. We left England in the hope of starting a new business here, but with no more money than we gave to the innkeeper there seems to be little hope of that, so we are looking for work, bookkeeping or something like it."

"We have seen many men like you, I wager that you have escaped the law back in England. Tell me or it might go badly for you." He nodded to the large man who held each of them by the arm with a surprisingly strong grip.

Robinson looked at Beadle who shrugged and nodded his head. "You are right, sir, we are wanted for theft, my wife's jewels which I bought for the ungrateful bitch. She has a powerful family and friends, so we had to run. The captain of a trading ship promised to take us to America, but he stole the jewels and dumped us ashore here. But I *am* a lawyer, sir."

The flinty eyes looked at each of them again for several minutes while he made up his mind. "I think that story may be true, you are felons and will be hanged if you are caught so you are desperate to start a new life here, am I not right?"

Both men nodded miserably, both worried that they might have fallen from the frying pan into the fire again.

"I will give you work on a casual basis until you have proved yourselves capable of keeping secrets. You, Robinson, if that's truly your name, if you really know the law I can use you. My partner was a lawyer, but he died over a year ago and that side of my business has almost disappeared. You will find his office upstairs with all you will need and another room up there with two rough beds where you can sleep. It's all dusty and dirty so the two of you can start right away cleaning it up.

"You, Beadle, will carry messages and documents for me to various places on the island, offices, plantations and private houses and the like. You are very lucky one of my two messengers fell off his horse and broke his neck last week. If you prove competent and useful, you will be well paid. You will start work tomorrow at dawn. My man Thomas will show you where you are to go. Remember, I could turn you both in to the authorities. No doubt there is a small reward."

Thomas led them back into the passage, thrust rags, a broom, a bucket and a pathetic string mop with half the strings missing into their hands and opened one of the two doors in the passage. This led to a stairway and another passage leading out to a yard at the back. Upstairs, Thomas showed them their rooms and told them that they would find a pump in the yard then left them to work.

Intriguingly the doors of the two other rooms were padlocked but they had no time for speculation as they immediately explored the two rooms. The room with two rough beds was small but adequate with straw mattresses and some grubby blankets. The office had a good-sized desk, chairs, a long shelf full of law books and a large cupboard stuffed with papers and ledgers. Everything was covered in dust and spider webs.

Beadle went down for water while Robinson started on the books with a dusting rag, surprised to find them almost new and a very good selection, invaluable to a lawyer. Beadle returned with the water, and they set to with a will, brushing, mopping, and dusting both rooms. Thomas re-appeared, took a good look round, grunted approval and gave them some polish.

"Mr Meyberg says you should polish everything and before you go, he will come up and see you."

Meyberg was grudgingly satisfied, gave them some money, and recommended that they should get the bedding to a woman he knew to be washed. They left the place, looking for a meal, relieved that they had found some kind of work but they both knew that they were now involved in something illegal.

Chapter Seventeen

Prisoners reveal the French land plot

Dawn was breaking with its usual rapidity when Merriman, Mr Graham and Doctor McBride arrived at the Admiral's offices the next day. They found Admiral Howarth in a jovial mood, plainly delighted by the results of the previous day's activities, although he frowned when he asked why Merriman had not brought his report last night.

"I apologise, sir, I did not finish writing my report until 10 o'clock and then my servant had to copy it, so I thought it not wise to disturb you at nearly midnight."

"Quite right, Captain, quite right. Your Lieutenant gave me your request but in future I want your report on my desk as soon as possible. I will read the details later but tell me briefly what happened. But first, I know Mr Grahame, but who is the other gentleman with you?"

"My apologies, air, this is Doctor McBride from..."

He was interrupted by the Admiral saying, "Ah, so this is the worthy doctor the Army is praising so much. You are welcome, Doctor. Now then, Mr Merriman, your report."

"Yes, sir, we looked into as many bays and inlets as we could but apart from a few small fishing boats we saw no privateers or pirates. We had no contact with the shore until we sailed into the bay next to Guiana Island when the ship was fired on from the shore. As the ship rounded a small headland I saw two small ships anchored ahead of me with men boarding. As the water was shallowing rapidly, I had to anchor and send a boarding party off to take them. Unfortunately, from where I was forced to anchor, the ship nearest to me shielded the first ship from my guns and, although I fired some shots and hit it, it managed to get away before my boarders could get to it. I couldn't follow, sir, because the water was too shallow. The two of them were cutters not drawing as much water as *Aphrodite*. If there had been another of our ships on the other side of Guiana Island, we might have caught both of them, sir," he said, greatly daring as if implying that the Admiral had been at fault.

"I know, Captain. I know I promised another of ours would go up the eastern side, but the sloop I was expecting didn't come in until this afternoon with the damage you will have seen. She found a privateer attacking a trading vessel, engaged it and sank it but lost her topmast and some men."

"I'm sorry about that, sir. We and the army captured some twenty-nine men and of course the one privateer which I hope the Navy will buy in."

"A bit of prize money for you, sir?" The Admiral looked at him with a smile on his face. "Indeed, Captain, you and your rogues will all get their share."

Merriman continued his report. "Colonel Shawcross was wounded but my doctor soon bandaged him up. Mr Grahame was with me and now he is desperate to know what may be learned from the prisoners."

"I imagine you are, sir, I imagine that you are. Well, Captain Blythe was here not ten minutes past giving me a verbal report. Colonel Shawcross is being a good patient and is resting with his leg up as you ordered, Doctor, but how long he will keep to his enforced inactivity I don't know. You had better go and see him."

"If you have finished with me, sir, I would like to go with the good doctor and Mr Grahame, to see the Colonel and to see what is being done with the prisoners and what we may learn from them," said Merriman.

"Very well then. Off you go, gentlemen."

At the army barracks they were ushered into the colonel's office to find him behind his desk, busily writing and with his leg up on a chair. Two other officers were with him and the one Merriman had met, Major Heath-Jones. After the introductions and all were seated, Merriman began, "Colonel, the Doctor wishes to examine your wound, sir, and Mr Grahame and I wish to know what information can be found out from the prisoners. Anything about French activities in the islands?"

"First of all, Captain, I want to thank the good Doctor for his ministrations. There is little pain now, Doctor, but I will rest my leg for another day or two as you instructed. And now to the matter of the prisoners, Major Heath-Jones can tell you everything."

"Well, Captain," responded the Major, "we have already sorted them out into three groups, the seven slaves are just that, escaped from the plantations and they will go into the slave pens until claimed or sold. Of the twenty two whites, eleven are French and the rest, another eleven of them, are English, deserters from your navy, sir."

"If they are deserters, sir, they must hang, unless they have a good reason, like the man Plover and his companion captured the other day, to be with Frenchmen and privateers. However, it will be up to the Navy to deal with them."

"I agree, Captain, and the eleven Frenchmen are being questioned as we speak. Our Sergeant Wrigley is a big man, well used to using his fists to keep order and is very persuasive, so I don't think we shall have to wait long."

Indeed, it was not long before a white-faced Lieutenant presented himself in the Colonel's office, followed by the big sergeant rubbing his knuckles, who stood to attention in a corner.

"We have, that is, Sergeant Wrigley has, made some of them talk, sir. We questioned them separately, sir, and from what we can gather they have a leader who managed to escape leaving the other ship in our hands. They call that man 'Le Seigneur.' They think he is French, but he can speak and behave like an Englishman and lives somewhere in Jamaica. He sends men to the islands to stir up the slaves with talk of revolution, freedom, and equality so that they will revolt and kill their owners. Have I missed anything, Sergeant?"

"No, sir, I don't think so, only that they think the man is a trader with many ships, sir," replied Wrigley, screwing up his face in concentration.

"That is all very interesting no doubt, but is there nothing else?" asked Grahame earnestly. "No mention of where else they are to go to spout their rubbish about equality, not that the slaves would be any better off?"

"No, sir, nothing, but I'm sure Sergeant Wrigley would be pleased to have another try." At those words, the sergeant smiled and rubbed his knuckles again.

"Leave them for an hour or so to think about it, Lieutenant, then you can try for more, Sergeant," said the Major. "We shall wait here for any more news."

When the men had gone Grahame quietly said, "I don't like the idea of beating prisoners, but I do think in this case that the ends justify the means. We now know a lot more than we did and hopefully we will know more in due course."

The Lieutenant was soon back. "We found out some more, gentlemen, but not a lot. Not until the Sergeant beat the three of them almost senseless, did they divulge anything else. They think that man 'Le Seigneur' wants to buy up those estates where the rightful owners are dead or have fled. He could buy them cheaply, I'm sure, sir," reported the Lieutenant.

"Thank you, Lieutenant, you may go. Have the prisoners fed and watered while we decide what to do with them?" asked the Colonel.

"Well, that gives us plenty to think about, James," said Grahame. "And now with your leave, Colonel, we must go back to the ship to think out our next move."

"Certainly, you may, gentlemen, but not before I urge you to accept Army hospitality this evening and the Doctor has examined my wound."

Chapter Eighteen

The French Plot Discussed

Merriman, Grahame, and the Doctor returned to *Aphrodite* where they settled in Merriman's cabin with freshly brewed coffee provided by Peters.

"Quite a well thought out plot, James, if all we have learned is true. Would you go over it again and give me your views?"

"Yes, sir, if the information is correct, and I emphasise the 'if', there is some French trader masquerading as an Englishman and living in Jamaica. He sends his bully boys along to plantations to encourage the slaves to revolt then, when the owners have been frightened off or killed, he can buy everything at a rock bottom price. I think he will then bring in his own overseers, settle the slaves down with violence if necessary and then carry on with what is now his own sugar production. He has his own ships to transport it to wherever he can sell it. I can think of nothing more, sir."

"Well done, James, your thoughts parallel my own exactly. Now we must decide what to do next, any ideas?"

"Not much beyond today, sir. The deserters must be handed over to the Admiral, but I would like to keep the man Plover and his mate. I did more or less promise him his life. As for the French, it is up to the army to deal with them, and the authorities here can investigate recent sales of plantations and to whom they were sold."

This all happened as expected. The marines escorted the deserters down to the shipyard where they were locked up to await the inevitable court martial when sufficient officers could be gathered together. Merriman had Plover and the other man taken aboard the *Aphrodite* as pressed men and the French prisoners were forced, in chains, to work on the construction of more fortifications.

A convivial evening followed at the army barracks to which the Admiral and all the naval officers were invited. There was only one sour note: the unpleasant and drunken Lieutenant Orson challenged Merriman to a duel, but the Colonel had him forcibly removed and urged Merriman to forget it if he would.

"The man's a fool, Mr Merriman, useless with a sword or pistol and I have no doubt you would quickly deal with him. But it was you the man challenged and if you feel you must accept his challenge, you can of course do so."

"Thank you, sir, but the man was drunk and hardly knew what he was doing so I am prepared to forget it."

"Very well then, I will deal with him tomorrow. Severely, you may rely on it."

It was in the early morning when they left the Colonel with their thanks for an excellent dinner. Dawn found *Aphrodite* well out to sea heading towards the next islands governed by Britain.

Chapter Nineteen

The Traitors put to work

The first work Robinson and Beadle were given was to sort out all the documents and ledgers in the cupboard. This was work Beadle was well suited for and he took charge, with Robinson fetching and carrying and cleaning them. They were mostly deeds, copies of property dealings, bills of sale, ship's manifests, estimates, valuations of cargoes of sugar and other goods, with a surprisingly big pile of letters and invoices relevant to the details and dates in the ledgers.

This took most of the day, but it was done at last, and Robinson went downstairs to tell Meyberg. Thomas admitted him again and Robinson found Meyberg in conversation with a man who was obviously a sailor. He was not introduced and quickly left.

Meyberg followed them upstairs, looked at the results of their work, expressed his satisfaction and asked if there was anything else they would need.

"Indeed yes, Mr Meyberg," replied Robinson. "I shall need suitable headed paper, ink and quills and sealing wax before we start."

"Very well, you shall have them. You will start again early tomorrow." He gave them some more money and left them.

Over a meal in a tavern, they discussed what they had done.

"It seems to be all the usual stuff one would expect in a lawyer's office all quite usual and above board," said Robinson. "But what I'd like to know is what is locked away in those other rooms."

Beadle sniffed. "No idea, but it may be something illegal, I'd gamble on it. We may get to know some time, but if we keep our master happy, he may trust us more."

And so, it went on. Meyberg disappeared regularly on his actuarial business, visiting clients and the like. His notes were given to Robinson and Beadle to transcribe into correct legal documents which were then entrusted to Beadle to deliver. A stable in the yard behind the office held two horses and eventually he was shown where these letters and documents were to go.

Time passed, days into weeks and they learned more about their employer. Meyberg used one of the locked rooms upstairs as his bedroom and Thomas acted as his bodyguard and servant. They knew that other heavily sealed letters were written by Meyberg and then dispatched by other messengers without being shown to Beadle. It became very obvious that Meyberg was deeply involved in some other dubious business as various strange characters visited at all times in the day and night. From upstairs they could hear men dragging things out of the one room they had not been allowed into and heaving them onto a wagons.

Certainly they were well paid. The money enabled them to purchase new, more suitable clothes for themselves and they began to eat at better places than the tavern they had first used. They were wise enough not to pry into any of Meyberg's other affairs and they had fitted their sleeping room with some new furniture and bedding. In short, life was almost idyllic. Memories of England and their crimes began to fade into insignificance, and they began to hope that they were safe.

How wrong they were. Nemesis was on its way aboard a Royal Naval sloop by the name of *Aphrodite*.

Chapter Twenty

Anguilla. The English Trader and the French Plot

Aphrodite was moving slowly with only a light and fickle wind to help her. Both Merriman and Mr Grahame fretted at the slowness of progress. Merriman spent hours on deck, alternatively tugging at his ear and squeezing the small, tightly-wrapped bundle of rags given to him by Helen's father - the good Doctor Simpson - to strengthen his damaged arm. That bundle took his mind back to thoughts of home, of Helen who had agreed to marry him when he returned, and of his family and his father's collection of old swords.

He remembered that it was his companion Grahame who had encouraged him to ask Helen to marry him and his surprise when she said yes. *It could be months, even years before we see each other again,* he mused gloomily. *She may have regretted agreeing, she may already have forgotten what I look like.* His frowning face kept everyone away from him, with all men except the Master and his mates at the wheel busy trying to look busy. With an effort, Merriman dragged his thoughts back to the present.

His seaman's instinct told him that the weather was changing. The day had been almost windless with only a few cat's paws on the surface of the sea. Now the wind was freshening a little and clouds were gathering on the eastern horizon. He turned to the Master, old Mr Cuthbert, whose knowledge of wind and waves around the world was second to none. "Looks as though we may be in for a blow, Master. What do you think?"

"Yes, sir, as you say. I'd have the tops'ls and t'gallants off her directly and may I propose a double reef in the courses."

"Yes, see to it if you please, Master."

Merriman beckoned the Officer of the Watch, Second Lieutenant Andrews to him and said, "David, we are in for some bad weather. Have all the gun lashings checked and make sure that the boats are secured properly and all hatches battened down. You know what must be done."

"Aye-aye, sir," replied Andrews cheerfully as he began to shout the necessary orders.

The Master already had Topmen aloft to reduce sail but in the few minutes since Merriman had first spoken, the sea was changing. The blue was becoming greyer, and the wind had risen even more and was backing northerly. The wind briefly lessened, then blew again with an exceptionally strong gust and one of the tops'ls not yet quite reefed fully, blew out with a noise of a musket shot.

Merriman saw a man fall from aloft into the sea with his mouth open in a scream and then he was gone, with no hope of the ship turning to rescue him in what was becoming a gale. The rain approached like a veritable wall of water. His man Owen appeared with Merriman's waterproofs. "Thought you might need these, sir. It's going to be wet."

Grahame suddenly appeared on deck clad in his own waterproofs and clinging on to everything he could.

"Mr Grahame, sir, you should be below, the weather is going to get worse."

"I will in a moment, James. I have remembered a quotation from Shakespeare which is suitable, and I couldn't wait to tell you. It's from Julius Caesar, I think, and is *'I have seen the tempests when the scolding winds have riv'd the knotty oaks and I have seen the ambitious ocean swell and rage and foam.'"*

"Very good, sir. Now I must insist that you go below and remember the old saying *'What cannot be cured must be endured.'* I'm sorry, but I am too busy to talk more."

Grahame vanished below, already a touch green in the face with his usual malady, sea sickness.

The gale quickly blew itself out and the blazing sun re-appeared in a cloudless blue sky almost as fast as the gale had risen. The wind was stronger than before the gale and, with all sail set, Merriman noted with satisfaction that the ship was able to progress much faster to its next port of call - St Kitts and Nevis. These were two small islands, volcanic with large central peaks covered in forest and well-watered. The land flattened out nearer the sea enough to support some small farms and plantations.

As *Aphrodite* approached the main harbour, all officers surveyed the land keenly through their telescopes and Merriman gave the order to Mr Laing to beat to quarters, to load the guns but to keep the port lids closed.

"We must be careful here, James," remarked Grahame. "We only took over this place ten years ago. For all I know the French may have taken it back again but even if not, there could be some French sympathisers left there."

"I quite agree, sir, which is why I have the men at their stations for action."

However, there was no difficulty. The union flag was clearly visible above a small fort on a slight eminence on the shoreline and people could be seen waving from the harbour wall.

Grahame and Merriman went ashore with a guard of marines and visited the English Governor, Sir Graham Dobson, who had no knowledge of any French activity on the islands. He was informed about their suspicions and requested that he investigate all plantation and land sales for the past few years.

"Nothing there, James," said Grahame as they were rowed back to the ship. "The next stop will be Anguilla to the north of here."

Once they were in the waters of Anguilla, they approached with care from the north, avoiding the various small islands and cays, to anchor in Crocus Bay overlooked by the capital known as the Valley. The island had been British owned for years, it was a pleasant island, cooled by the northeast trade winds and they received a warm welcome from the Governor. Over refreshment they asked if he had any information about possible French interference on the island, and sales or changes of ownership of land which might be significant.

"I can tell you that in few minutes, my secretary will know," said the Governor, turning to shout, "Brougham, Brougham, where are you?"

A small man almost tumbled into the room such was his haste. "Yes, sir, what can I do?"

The Governor told him what his visitors had asked about. Brougham screwed up his face in concentration, thought for a few moments then said, "I believe there was one, only perhaps two months ago. The owners, Mr and Mrs White, left here in poor health and went back to England. As usual we sent notification to all British possessions that it was up for sale, and I think it sold very quickly, sir. I can't remember who bought it but if you will give me a moment I can find out."

He soon returned to the room with a heavy ledger and various papers. "I've found it, sir. The plantation, very run down it was, was sold to an English trader name of Simon Edgerton from Jamaica. He uses a lawyer in Kingston, a Mr Isaac Meyberg. The money was sent here and then to the White's bank in England. The documentation was all in perfect order, sir."

He ran his finger down an earlier record, raised his eyebrows, and said, "Strange, there is another one, sir. The owner, Mr Burton, suddenly put his property on the market and also left for England. In both cases the properties sold for under the expected prices and both to the same man, the trader from Jamaica."

"Thank you, Brougham. I hope that is what you wanted, gentlemen?"

"Indeed yes, sir," replied Grahame. "I think we will find that information most useful."

The Governor invited them to stay and have dinner with himself and his wife and to stay there for the night. They gratefully accepted the invitation to dinner but declined to stay.

"Sorry, sir," replied Merriman, "but we must proceed to our next destination very early in the morning so we must decline your kind invitation to stay. In any event I must be aboard my ship, but with many thanks for your hospitality, sir."

"Oh dear, my wife will be disappointed. She hoped to hear more about the fashions in London and all that sort of feminine nonsense, but I quite understand. The King's business cannot be delayed."

And so, with 'Best Wishes' and 'God Speed' ringing in their ears they departed. Once aboard, Merriman issued orders for the ship to be got under way at first light, bound back to Antigua.

Chapter Twenty-One

Old friends meet. More details of French plot

Arriving at English Harbour again, and after all the usual gun signals completed, both Merriman and Grahame made their way to Admiral Howarth's office, still cool under the shade of the palm trees.

"Welcome back, gentlemen, sit down, please, sit down. May I offer you some refreshments? After you left, we found out some information on land and property sales. One plantation is currently in the process of being sold, the final documents are on their way to Jamaica in the hands of a representative of a lawyer there, but the money has been paid. A farm was also sold months ago to the same man, a Mr Edgerton, a trader from Jamaica. It seems that he acquired them at rock bottom prices."

Merriman and Grahame looked at one another significantly before Grahame nodded and said, "That seems to agree with our suspicions, James, don't you think?"

Merriman nodded. "It would seem so, sir, and now that we have more information than we had from the French prisoners last time, Admiral, may we be permitted to question them again? I think we now know what more questions we need answers for."

"Certainly, you may. I'll have the Army take them down from the new fort where they are working, into the barracks where they can be dealt with as before."

A servant was dispatched to make the arrangements and before very long a soldier arrived to inform them that the prisoners were now at the barracks waiting to be questioned. Merriman and Grahame walked there and were ushered into the Colonel's office. He came forward to greet them, limping a little but using a walking cane.

"Welcome, gentlemen, it's a pleasure to see you again. Sit down, you will take some refreshment I'm sure." He sat and grinned over his desk at Merriman. "Got a surprise for you, Captain. Come in, Captain Saville."

The door opened and Merriman turned to see none other than his friend Robert Saville, whom he had not seen since the last time he was at home.

Merriman leapt to his feet and thrust out his hand. "By God, Robert, it's good to see you again."

They shook hands, grinning at each other like a pair of Cheshire cats. Robert was dressed in the regimentals of the 22nd Regiment of Foot, the red coat with buff and gold facings, as he had been when they first met on a coach from London to Chester at the end of last year. The two of them and Mr Grahame had met at a coaching inn where Merriman had been instrumental in saving them from a number of card cheats. Grahame smiled and shook hands with the soldier. "A pleasure to meet you again, Captain. Maybe we shall see more of you."

Colonel Shawcross interrupted, "Gentlemen, this is all very good, but we do have a serious matter in hand, your reminiscences can come later. You asked if you could question the prisoners again and they are waiting in the cells for you with our Sergeant Wrigley."

"Good," exclaimed Grahame. "I will go and talk to them and you, James, why don't you stay and catch up with your old friend?"

Outside and walking in the welcome shade of the palm trees, Merriman and Saville could hardly contain themselves and both tried to talk at once until Merriman held up his hand for silence. "Now then, Robert, I can see that *you* are well but please tell me about my family."

"Both your parents are well, James, and so is your brother." He paused for effect and then said, "And your sister Emily." He paused again.

"Yes, yes, man, what about my sister, is she well?" demanded Merriman, in a fever to know what might be wrong at home.

"Oh, she is very well, James, very well indeed." Saville looked sheepishly at his friend and then the news came out in a rush. "I asked her to marry me, James, and she did me the honour of accepting me, I hope you will appro …"

He broke off as Merriman pounded him on his back and shouted delightedly, "Of course I approve, Robert! I'm pleased for you both, now tell me all about it."

"Well, I knew somehow from the time I first met her, when you invited me to your family home, that I was strongly attracted to her. I visited your home several times while you have been away, James, to see them all, especially Emily. I could see that she was attracted to me so I asked them if I could ask her to marry me. Your father questioned me at some length about my family and prospects and then he agreed, but the wedding will have to wait for now. I love her dearly, James, and you may be sure that I will look after her to the best of my ability."

"I know you will, Robert. Even I could see the way you looked at each other and I wondered what might happen. Anyway, I see Mr Grahame is waiting to see me and you will have your duties to attend to, so I must go. With your Colonel's approval I will send a boat for you later and you can join me and my officers aboard at dinner this evening."

Back aboard *Aphrodite* and seated in the main cabin with coffee prepared by the ever-ready Peters, Merriman and Grahame discussed what had been learned from further interrogation of the French prisoners.

"It was amazing what I heard, James. That big sergeant was with me, looking as though he wanted to be let loose on them again and with that implied threat they couldn't answer fast enough. There was little new but one of them told me that he thought the man they called 'Le Seigneur' was from Jamaica and owned a lot of trading vessels. What was new is that 'Le Seigneur' owns three fast, well-armed ships as well to protect his own trading ships. I think it is possible that they could be privateers in their spare time. We were told last time that it was thought that the man was a Frenchman masquerading as an Englishman and if that is true he could be working as a spy. Certainly, his trade ships sailing between the islands would be ideal for landing men to stir up the slaves and pass messages about British activities back to Jamaica. One of the prisoners thought 'Le Seigneur' was named Edge or something like it. What do you think, James?"

"It seems to me, sir, that following the comment from one of our first prisoners that all was going well in Jamaica, that we must go and see what we can find out there. If I may suggest it, we could go early in the morning after we have entertained Colonel Shawcross, Major Heath-Jones, and Captain Saville on board for dinner." Merriman then told Grahame the news about his family, whom Grahame had met, his sister and Saville.

"That is most excellent news, James. I agree, we must have a good dinner to celebrate."

"Thank you, sir. I will send invitations ashore right away."

That night, the visitors arrived and introductions made, although some of Merriman's officers already knew Captain Saville since the events in the Irish Sea. So, cramped though they were in Merriman's cabin, still hot although doors and windows were wide open, they enjoyed a feast of chicken, pork and all the trimmings, cheese, and wine from his own stock, all served competently by Peters and two seamen conscripted to help.

After the Loyal Toast and the table had been cleared, they were all settled with coffee and brandy when Merriman rapped on the table for quiet and said, "Gentlemen, I have an announcement to make. Some of you have met my family and I am happy to tell you that my sister Emily has accepted Captain Saville's proposal of marriage."

His voice was almost drowned out by the noise and commotion following that announcement. All wanted to shake Saville by the hand, pound him on the back and wish him well. As a bemused and happy Saville subsided into his seat Merriman said, "Gentlemen and friends, I would like to propose a toast to the couple and especially to Robert who is here with us, so please raise your glasses. To Robert and Emily. We wish them all happiness in their future together."

More noise arose as all tried to talk at once and Merriman knew that the news would be round the ship in no time. "Peters, more brandy, hurry yourself, man."

And so, the party broke up after a great evening and the visitors left, some of them, including Saville, somewhat fuddled from the wine and brandy but still able to thank Merriman for his hospitality. Saville, swaying gently on his feet said, "James, I hope to see you again before too long, but I have to leave here with some of the recruits. I don't know where to or how many will be alive in a year or so. The death rate here from fevers is enormous."

"I know, Robert. My ship's doctor has learned a lot about medicine from Helen's father who spent years in India in the tropics. Good ventilation is one thing and keep away from the locally brewed rum. I shall have the good doctor write down all he can, and I'll send it to you in the morning. So, goodnight and take care."

Chapter Twenty-Two

The Traitors Threatened by Frenchman

Meanwhile back in Jamaica, Robinson and Beadle were congratulating themselves on their good fortune. Meyberg did little to have the premises cleaned up, but a newly painted sign was erected outside proudly announcing the new Legal Services. Both of them had become very useful and Robinson especially was beginning to make a name for himself as a good lawyer. Beadle was becoming used to the town and surrounding area from carrying messages for Meyberg. Both were quite well paid and becoming accustomed to their new circumstances.

One evening as they left the office, a roughly dressed man stepped out of an alley and confronted them, saying in an unmistakable French accent, "Don't I know you?"

"I don't think so," replied Robinson.

"Oh, don't come all innocent with me, I know both of you, better than you may think. I was in Paris with M'sieur Moreau, and I saw you many times bringing him messages and reporting to him. You were part of his spy ring in Ireland, weren't you?"

"Yes, I was," mumbled Robinson. "We had to get away and we came here to find work."

"Well, I won't denounce you, you can work for us. You speak good French, and you are more presentable than you were when you arrived. Oh yes, I saw you the day you arrived here. We can make use of you both. You'll soon be able to travel freely as you did in Ireland and help us in many ways."

"Is Moreau here in Jamaica?" asked Beadle hesitantly.

"Not yet, but I wouldn't be surprised if he was or coming soon. Now be off with you for your dinner, I'll be in touch. Don't forget: you will be watched."

As they sat over their meal, a despondent Beadle asked "What do we do now then, tell me that? We left England and jumped out of the frying pan into the fire and now it seems that we are in another frying pan. So I repeat, what do we do now?"

"I cannot be sure, Beadle, but from what that man said it seems we are caught between him and French spies and Meyberg and his activities which we believe to be smuggling. I think we shall have to wait and see and save as much money as we can, maybe to buy a way out of here!"

Chapter Twenty-Three

To Jamaica. Privateers Captured

The *Aphrodite* was making her way to Jamaica, purposefully keeping well away from the Spanish held islands of Puerto Rico and Dominica. As Grahame commented, "We don't know if they are our allies or if they have gone over to the French, so we had best stay clear."

The voyage of about one thousand miles would take several days dependant on the weather, and routine aboard was proceeding normally. Every day the men practiced sail changing, reefing and setting, gunnery and what to do for every eventuality Merriman could think of. With the wind behind them it was much cooler, and he and Grahame spent long hours on deck reading their favourite Shakespeare plays, although Merriman was always alert to what was happening around him. Continually they discussed what they should do when they reached Jamaica but all they knew for certain were the names of some of the men involved in buying plantations cheaply after the owners had left.

One day as the ship lay becalmed, a lookout aloft shouted, "Deck there, I can see smoke on the horizon, maybe gun smoke, sir, and I think I can hear gunfire too."

"Up you go, Mr Shrigley, tell me what you see," said Merriman.

"Nothing more, sir," yelled Shrigley in his usual squeaky voice which was beginning to break. "Just smoke and gunfire, sir, but I can see a sail off to starboard. Can't identify it yet, sir."

"Very good, Mr Shrigley, come down now." He turned to the officer of the watch, the First Lieutenant Colin Laing. "Mr Laing, beat to quarters, but don't load the guns and don't show our colours just yet."

Laing shouted the orders, and the rattle of the little drummer boy's small drum was heard as the men scrambled up from below and to their usual places. Some at the guns with their officers and others on deck by the masts waiting for the order to shorten sail.

"Have the men stand easy at their quarters, Mr Laing. With this lack of wind we can't investigate any further. Send Larkin aloft to join the other man, maybe his better eyes can tell us more."

After a half an hour Larkin shouted, "Deck there, the ship to starboard is closing, sir, he must have some wind over there."

"Thank you, Larkin, keep your eye on it and keep me informed."

For almost an hour nothing changed until a gentle breeze arrived and the ship began to move forward again. Larkin shouted down, "Can' hear any more gunfire, sir, but there is still a lot of smoke and the ship to starboard is moving closer, sir."

Merriman desperately wanted to see for himself so, seizing one of the ship's telescopes, he swung himself into the shrouds and climbed up to the mainmast crosstrees. He opened the glass but wanted to see even more so he climbed even higher to the topmast crosstrees where a very surprised Larkin moved over to give him room to open his glass again. "Has anything changed?" he asked.

"No, sir, not that I can see but if you would lend me the glass, sir, I might do better. Yes, sir, the smoke and gunfire must 'ave come from one ship on its own. I thought there must 'ave been two of 'em fighting but the smoke fooled me, sir. There is still smoke, sir, and the other ship to starb'd is nearer now."

Merriman had seen enough, he quickly regained the quarterdeck and beckoned Lieutenant Laing, the Master, the marine Lieutenant, and midshipman Oakley to join him. "I don't know for certain, gentlemen, but I have the feeling that we have sailed into a trap. The lookout thought there were two ships fighting ahead, but all he could see was smoke and now we can see only one ship ahead giving out a lot of smoke but no gunfire. It appears to be a small merchant vessel. As you can see the other ship to starboard is closing rapidly. Fortunately, the wind is rising so we shall be able to manoeuver easily. This is what I propose. First, I'll have the guns loaded but keep the ports closed until we are nearer. Second, Mr Cuthbert, I want you to steer directly to the windward side of the ship ahead and if we time it right then the other ship will be almost upon us..."

The crash of gunfire interrupted him. The ship astern had fired its bowchasers in warning, the balls splashing alongside.

"Very good, they have declared themselves then. They must think we are simply another trading ship. Mr Laing, just before they reach us, run out the guns and give it a broadside. Is that all clear, gentlemen? Mr Oakley, go and present my compliments and tell the officers at the guns what is expected of them, then come back here. Mr St James, have your men hide behind the nettings until we open fire. I don't want the sight of red coats to scare them away. We officers must hide our coats, blue uniform coats could also give warning."

With the following wind, *Aphrodite* rapidly closed with the ship ahead and as Merriman had predicted, the smoke ceased, and a flood of men appeared on deck. They undoubtedly were privateers.

"Steady as she goes, Master. Mr Shrigley, be ready to hoist our colours when I say." Merriman watched the gap keenly and also the ship closing rapidly astern, then shouted, "Mr Andrews, prepare to open fire and Mr Shrigley, colours aloft."

The surprise seemed to be complete. Both ships tried to bear away but too late. As *Aphrodite* passed between them, Merriman roared "Fire." The broadsides tore into them, inflicting terrible damage and carnage among the men on the decks while the marines joined in with their muskets.

"Bring her about, Mr Laing, and we'll give them some more."

With the keen and eager crew pulling and hauling at the sheets and braces and the Master's Mates on the wheel, the ship seemed to turn on the spot and then head back to the privateers. As they moved to pass between the two damaged ships, Merriman could see streams of blood running down their sides before gun smoke hid the grisly sight.

As the wind blew the smoke away, Merriman shouted, "Mr Laing, have our carronades fire as we come nearer and then a full broadside if you please, and make sure you have boarding parties ready."

It was enough; a white cloth was waved from one of the battered ships.

"Mr Laing, prepare to board."

In no time *Aphrodite* crashed alongside the second ship and Laing led his men over to it. A few minutes later he waved and shouted that all was well, the crew had surrendered, and the small powder room secured.

"Very good, stay there while I go and see what the other is doing."

It was immediately obvious that the ship was in a bad way and Merriman ordered, "Mr Gorman, take a party of men over to her and take possession of her."

The 'her' was a brig, lightly laden by the way it rolled in the slight sea movement and Merriman realised that the privateers had thought his ship to be a trader and her cargo would have been transferred to the brig. Aboard the brig there was devastation, splintered timbers and dead and injured men. Gorman was first aboard with his marines and quickly shouted that the ship was theirs.

"Mr Gorman, I'm going to come over," shouted Merriman. He found the remaining crew sitting on the deck with their hands on their head and guarded by the marines.

"That's all of them, sir. A sullen looking lot, I think. There is nobody below and there is no powder magazine," reported Gorman. "They must have started the smoke in those three iron cauldrons to fool us."

"Well done, Mr Gorman, keep the men here, I'm going below to see if there are any documents in the cabin which might help us."

"I've already done that, sir," he said, grinning all over his face. He turned to a nearby seaman carrying a bag. "It's all in the bag, sir, at least all I could find."

Merriman took hold of the bag which was surprisingly heavy. "You seem to have thought of everything, William, but have you checked the holds?"

"Yes, sir, they're empty apart from ballast, but I don't think she will stay afloat for long. She's making water fast and the pumps don't work."

"In that case, Mr Gorman, put as many as you can into your boat and take them across to the *Aphrodite* where I suggest you put half of the prisoners in it with marines on guard. Then send the boat back to pick up the rest of them."

"Aye-aye, sir. At once," replied Gorman. That done, Merriman had himself rowed over to the other ship.

"There are only a few of the crew left, sir," reported Laing when Merriman climbed aboard to survey the situation. "We piled the bodies out of the way in case you want to say a few words over them before we tip them over the side. Regarding the ship, sir, if we can find a spare spar to fish to the stump of the mast, there are enough yards, sails, and ropes aboard to suit. We looked, sir, but there are no undamaged timbers aboard big enough to use as a mast."

"I'll float our spare mainyard over to you with some more men and Midshipman Oakley, but first, have you found any documents below?"

"Yes, sir, only a few although there is a small strong box for which there is no key. Perhaps the Captain threw it overboard but he's dead so…" He shrugged his shoulders.

"Right, Colin, have it put in the boat if you will. As for the bodies," here Merriman hardened his heart, "I will say nothing over them. They are no better than pirates so tip them over. When your prize is ready we'll make our way to Kingston."

The thought of prize money made Laing smile. "That will come in handy, sir, I'm sure."

Back aboard the *Aphrodite*, Merriman arranged for some more men to go over to the ship with Midshipman Oakley, the Bos'n and the Carpenter, towing the spare spar behind. Then, he called Grahame to his cabin and over a welcome drink they discussed what had occurred. The bag full of papers yielded little of interest, bills of lading, crew roster and lists of money spent.

"I think all this belonged to the original captain, sir, from before the privateers took her," surmised Merriman. "But here is one item of interest, a ship's manifest with the heading 'Egerton, General Trader'. That will give us a reason to visit this Egerton, don't you think?"

"You are right, James, it will, so let us look at the stuff from the second ship. None of them have names I suppose?"

"No, sir, all painted out, but from these papers, the brig seems to be *The Jamaican Traveller.*"

The few papers from the other ship revealed nothing of interest so their attention turned to the small strongbox. The box was very heavy, and the size of the keyhole indicated that a big key had been used.

"It will take a skilled locksmith to open that, James," said Grahame. "It will have to wait until we get to Kingston."

As they sat gazing glumly at the box they heard the thump of a boat alongside and moments later there came a knock on the cabin door.

"Come in," said Merriman, and an excited Midshipman Oakley appeared.

"Mr Laing's compliments, sir, and he found this key hidden in the cabin," he said excitedly.

"Excellent, Mr Oakley, now wait there, and we'll see if it fits this lock." It did, and Merriman flung the lid open. Inside there were more papers and another box taking up most of the space.

They looked at it in silence, with young Oakley straining to see what he could from behind his betters.

"Thank you, Mr Oakley. Go back to Lieutenant Laing, present my compliments and thanks and tell him that the key does fit," said Merriman with a smile.

A sudden shout of, "She's going," caused them to hurry up on deck in time to see the brig, whose stem was already under water, slide forward and disappear with only a great burst of bubbles and a ring of corpses to mark the spot.

Chapter Twenty-Four

Kingston, Jamaica

Aphrodite sailed into Kingston harbour under reduced sail followed by the prize ship with Lieutenant Laing in command. They anchored as the harbourmaster's boat directed and then the usual and required salutes were fired. A big two decker with an Admiral's flag aloft was anchored nearby with two frigates and several smaller craft. On the other side of the harbour was a large ship flying the American flag and near to it were two small sloops and a bigger ship, like a small frigate really, which Merriman recognised to be the style of the French corvette they had fought with in the Irish Sea. Hardly had *Aphrodite's* anchor splashed down when Midshipman Shrigley called, "Signal, sir, our number and Captain to report to Flag immediately."

Merriman's gig was already in the water. Gorman and Merriman climbed down into the boat and they were off to the flagship with the seamen tugging madly at the oars at Merriman's cox'n's urgings. Stepping through the entry port they were met by an ageing Captain. "I am Heathcliffe, gentlemen, Flag Captain to Admiral Hawkesby. Follow me if you will."

From the first they felt at home. The Admiral's great cabin had none of the female fripperies or high-quality mahogany furniture often found in such quarters, but it was plain and almost spartan. Heathcliffe introduced the two visitors and stood by while Admiral Hawkesby, a tall, lean figure of a man with heavily sunburnt features, welcomed them warmly. "Welcome aboard, gentlemen," he said, eyeing them closely.

Of course, Merriman was wearing his best uniform, but Grahame was simply dressed in his civilian clothes and was the subject of a longer and questioning look from the Admiral. Merriman hastened to introduce Grahame as a representative of Mr Pitt, the Prime Minister.

"You are welcome, sir," said the Admiral. "And what brings you to Jamaica?"

Grahame explained briefly why they were there and then showed him their various documents.

"Hmm, that all seems quite clear so what can I do to assist you?"

Merriman answered, "First of all, sir, two privateers attacked my ship, foolishly as it turned out. We sank one, a small brig and captured the other which is a small French-built corvette. The mast will need replacing; we fished it to our spare mainyard, sir. Most of the crews of both were killed but we have some prisoners, most of them American, some French and two English deserters, who must come ashore. Perhaps the Americans can be put aboard that American ship on the other side of the harbour, sir. We found various papers aboard and a steel strongbox which has given Mr Grahame some valuable information. It is all detailed in my report, sir." He handed the report over to the Admiral.

"May I know what was in the box, Mr Merriman?" he asked.

Grahame interrupted, "There is no harm in you knowing, sir, but I think that all we have found should also be seen by the Governor as much of it incriminates certain people here."

"I see, well if it is a civilian matter I don't need to know unless it affects my command. The Governor's offices are behind the main quayside, and he should be there at this time of day. If not, he will be at his home higher up the hill. Referring back to the prize you brought in, if it is in good order, I will arrange for the Navy to buy it, we can always use good small craft for all sorts of jobs. How many guns does it carry?"

"Only six nine-pounders, sir, my ship's armament completely overwhelmed it, two broadsides killed most of the crews and they didn't put up much of a fight."

"Very well then. America is now at peace with us, and I don't want to be involved in any punishment the men may suffer. Captain Heathcliffe, please arrange for an officer to go with these gentlemen to introduce them to the Governor. Goodbye, gentlemen, I hope I shall have the pleasure of inviting you to dinner soon."

Heathcliffe took them up on deck and deputed Lieutenant Graves to accompany them to the Governor. Merriman's boat was still alongside and very quickly put them ashore on a strong stone-built quay, from where Graves took them into an imposing building with the union flag flying above it. A servant appeared and Graves told him that the Admiral had sent these visitors, and could they see the Governor at once? The servant scurried off, returning almost at once to usher them into the Governor's office, leaving Graves to wait in the entrance hall.

Governor Sir George Scarrow was an elderly and a corpulent man, obviously well used to the delights of the table and he welcomed them genially, immediately asking the servant to arrange refreshment for his guests. He asked them about their voyage, their health and what news they could tell him about London, laughing uproariously at some of the anecdotes Grahame related to him. Refreshments arrived and were distributed, then an immediate change came over Sir George. His joviality disappeared and his face became serious as he sternly asked them their business.

Both Merriman and Grahame showed him their orders and documents which he perused carefully before saying, "I would know Mr Pitt's signature anywhere. I have known him well from years past. So, what brings you to my little fiefdom?"

They explained that their principal reason was a trail of bits of information that had led them to Jamaica. The prisoners taken in Antigua, the news in Antigua and Anguilla, and the news in both about cheap land sales to a trader from Jamaica. Then they told him about the captured privateers and what they had found aboard.

"That strongbox is in my boat at the quay, sir, could you send Lieutenant Graves to ask my men to bring it here?"

Two sweating sailors carried the heavy box in and placed it on the floor, whereupon the governor ordered his servant to give them something to drink.

"No alcohol, sir, if you don't mind," said Merriman. "After you men have had your drink, then you can go back to the boat and take Lieutenant Graves back to the Flagship then come back here."

"Aye- aye, sir, thank you sir," said one of them, knuckling his forehead.

Merriman produced the key and opened the box with a flourish. Grahame spread the documents and papers on the desk and then indicated that the Governor should look into the box which was half filled with gold coins and a few items of jewellery. For a moment, the Governor stared, speechless then he asked, "This all came from that privateer, did it, and what do these papers tell us?"

"With what we already know, sir, quite a lot," replied Grahame. "If I could tell you exactly in detail what we do know it all seems to fit together. In Antigua and Anguilla, we found out that land had changed hands in unusual circumstances, and all bought at very low prices by a Jamaican trader. Prisoners we took were persuaded to talk, many of them were Frenchmen and they told us that they were sent to various islands by a man they called 'Le Seigneur' to try and make the plantation slaves revolt and force the real owners out. That piece of news decided us to come to Jamaica. We also learned that a lawyer by the name of Meyberg handles all the paperwork for the sales and pays the money over by his agent."

"My God! I knew that French agents must be here but who is this trader?"

"I'll come to that in a moment, Governor. We also learned that this trader is wealthy and has a small fleet of armed ships to escort his own trading vessels. Our capture of the privateer and the contents of this box encourages the belief that he uses those ships to act as privateers when not on escort duties."

"I am astounded, gentlemen. I know that lawyer Meyberg; he is a money lender, an actuary, and has long been suspected of dealing with stolen and smuggled goods. He has his fingers in all sorts of dubious pies and as I say, he has been long suspected but without proof I could do nothing. And the trader, who is he?"

"The papers we found on the smaller ship were mostly normal trading papers, bills of sale and such with the same trader's name on many of them. The papers in front of you sir reveal more. They refer to a man called 'Le Seigneur' and it is my belief that that man and the trader is in fact one and the same person, and that man is a Simon Egerton."

"Egerton? Egerton? I cannot believe it of him. No, no, you must be wrong. He is a well-respected member of our community, generous to a fault and a more than generous host. He is known to everybody who is anybody here, and welcomed anywhere. No, I cannot believe it."

"Nevertheless, we are convinced but, of course we can't accuse him face to face as yet, we need some more direct proof, Governor, and I think the place to start is with the lawyer Meyberg."

"Right, gentlemen, I will keep an open mind, but you can be sure that nothing of what you have told me will be repeated. I am holding a small reception at my house tomorrow evening. Egerton and his wife will be there, and I urge you to come along with some of your officers. Admiral Hawkesby is already invited, and you can see Egerton for yourselves. Come to think of it, Egerton holds many small evening dinners for his friends and acquaintances and that would give him plenty of opportunity to learn what is going on."

"Yes, sir, thank you, but as for the gold, the navy captured it so do we keep it, or should it be kept in your strongbox?"

"I will keep it for now, gentlemen, but I will give you a letter and receipt to confirm that."

Chapter Twenty-Five

An elegant and surprising party

As he was rowed back to the ship, Merriman saw that most of the men were staring at the town and natural harbour, drinking in the view. Kingston was surrounded by high land, the Blue Mountains, Long Mountain, and the Red Hills. The town itself had many brick or stone buildings and scores of white painted timber buildings. Climbing back aboard, Merriman harshly demanded to know if nobody had anything to do. The First Lieutenant apologised and shouted to the Warrant Officers to get the men back to work.

"I'm sorry, sir, but it is such a lovely view and most of the men are wondering if they will get any shore leave."

"I think so, Lieutenant, but only if all the usual work is completed and why are the awnings and wind sails not rigged?"

"I'm sorry, sir, my fault. I too was taking in the view. I'll have it done at once," said the startled man.

Below, Merriman and Grahame sat in his cabin to discuss what they had learned. "Well, James, we seem to be no further ahead than we were before. We must go to the Governors' reception tomorrow evening to be able to meet the man Egerton. Maybe we are wrong about him," said Grahame dolefully. "I don't know what else to do."

"It's difficult, sir, but I have one or two ideas which may help. I shall be letting parties of reliable men ashore at different times to give them a chance to enjoy themselves. If each group has a senior man with it, they can visit different taverns as you did in Antigua, and perhaps they will hear some French spoken. The senior man can report back to me. Also, you will remember Jackson who was with you on your adventure in Antigua. I suggest that we give him and the Gunner Salmon the task of watching the premises of lawyer Meyberg during the evening and overnight. They are both ex-poachers and may see or hear something to help us."

"Yes indeed, James, I know that Jackson can move in the dark like a cat."

And so it was arranged. The men were told that they would be going ashore the next day but only if the ship was in good order, clean decks, everything in its place and not a single rope's end loose. The men worked in a frenzy to be sure that nothing would be found wanting when the captain inspected the ship, which he did, looking everywhere before expressing himself satisfied.

Groups of excited men were sent ashore with instructions to visit as many taverns as they could to see what they might learn but with the strict reminder that if any man became totally drunk or involved with the local whores he would be very severely dealt with.

Salmon and Jackson also went ashore separately to find Meyberg's offices. They reported back later. "Sir, we found the place of the lawyer, sir. It's in Ship Road and looks filthy. Not what you expect for a lawyer's place, sir, but it's got a new sign board."

"Very well then, both of you, rest now until this evening and then I want you to watch the place and take note of who or what comes in or out, all night if necessary, and early morning too. Here is some money, you can take it in turn to find food somewhere."

That evening, Merriman together with Lieutenants Laing and Andrews, all in their best uniforms, carefully brushed, shoes and swords brightly polished until they gleamed, were rowed ashore in the cutter with Mr Grahame. Other officers, Lieutenant St James, Mr Cuthbert, and Midshipman Shrigley also went ashore with the express intention of finding a reputable place where they could find a good meal.

The Governor's house was not far to walk but it was slightly uphill, and they were glad to reach it. A black footman let them in and asked them to wait a moment, giving them the opportunity to quickly check their uniforms. Another servant appeared, a white man this time who asked their names. He led them to a large pair of doors behind which they could hear excited chatter and laughter, flung them open and announced in a loud voice, "The Officers of the Royal Navy, sir."

Polite applause greeted his words, and the Governor came forward to meet them. Merriman introduced Laing and Andrews, a servant proffered a tray of drinks, and they were soon in the middle of the party which appeared to be of about fifty people. Each of his officers was soon surrounded by gentlemen and their ladies all eagerly wanting to know what the fashionable ladies in London were wearing and what was the latest scandal and gossip.

Merriman spotted Admiral Hawkesby and his Flag Captain in deep conversation with two army officers resplendent in red and gold. Merriman had instructed his officers not to reveal why they were here, just to reply vaguely that they were here to reinforce Admiral Hawkesby's squadron.

The Governor himself with his wife took Merriman in hand and proceeded to introduce him to many of the guests before Merriman laughingly asked him to slow down, "I'll never remember all these names, sir."

The man smiled at him, "I am sure there are one or two more that you would like to meet, ah, here is Mr Simon Egerton, his lovely wife Isabella and her father Don Carlos Galiano."

The introductions made, the men bowed, the ladies curtseyed. Egerton's wife was a strikingly beautiful lady of above average height with a complexion hinting at mixed blood somewhere in her ancestry. Both Egerton and his wife immediately started asking the usual questions about London with Merriman racking his brains to remember details of London fashion. Strangely Don Carlos took no part in the conversation, contenting himself with listening.

"Are you in Jamaica for any particular reason, Captain Merriman, sir," asked Egerton. "We know that the navy is stretched to the limit keeping up its patrols all around the islands and trying to protect our convoys but what will you be expected to do?"

"I really cannot say, sir, we arrived only yesterday, and I have not yet received my orders from the Admiral," answered Merriman non-committedly.

Mrs Egerton broke in and said, "Oh, Simon, don't bother the poor man with questions like that. He is here to get away from thoughts of duty and enjoy himself. Captain Merriman, I see that the refreshments are ready, perhaps you would be kind enough to escort me in?"

He caught the brief flash of a strange look between her and her husband but thought no more about it at the time. The heat was almost overpowering, and he felt perspiration trickling down his sides beneath his heavy coat. He was determined not to take too much alcohol to drink and so when he found glass jugs of orange and pineapple juice he drank thirstily.

The food was arranged on several large tables and the guests were able to move all round them to select their own choices from the finger buffet. Isabella kept offering him small items to eat but he said that he didn't normally eat a lot and contented himself with portions of chicken, meat, and fish although some of it was so highly spiced that he found himself drinking even more orange juice. He glanced around and saw his officers, each with a heaped plate and obviously enjoying themselves.

"Have you had enough, dear Captain? I am faint with this heat so would you take me out for some fresh air?" asked Mrs Egerton. She indicated a pair of doors leading out to a terrace where she breathed heavily and fanned herself gently before taking his arm and almost dragging him further.

Poor Merriman, he was almost sure the deep breathing was to draw attention to her fine, barely concealed breasts and when he felt her breast pushing against his arm he was sure. She wanted to seduce him, perhaps to learn more about him and his reason for being in Jamaica.

In a gloomy corner of the garden, she suddenly swung to face him, flung her arms around his neck, and kissed him hard. Shocked, he said, "I'm married, Isabella, you're married, we shouldn't be doing this." He was not yet married but he hoped that the thought would slow down her advances.

In that he was mistaken. She took his hand and pulled it to her breasts, which she had uncovered. "Don't worry about that, Captain, my husband doesn't and it's a long time since I had a real man."

Merriman felt his body begin to respond but determined not to fall under her spell he said firmly, "I thank you for all that you are offering, Isabella, but I love my wife and I can't help you. I think it is time we went back to the party."

"Damn you, Captain, you've got me all excited now, but I hope we may have another chance." She pulled her dress back up, took his arm and led him back to the house.

Her husband was standing close by in conversation with the Governor and Merriman saw her give the merest shake of her head as she looked at him.

Pulling himself together, Merriman turned to the Governor to thank him and as they moved towards the door he said, "A lovely evening, sir, I thank you and your wife, and now I must collect my people and return to my ship. I must go and see that all is in order before I turn in."

"Thank you for coming, Captain, I hope you found what you were looking for."

"Maybe, sir, maybe," he replied as he caught the eyes of Laing and Grahame, signifying that they should go.

As they passed the Admiral, he beckoned Merriman and ordered him to report to the Flagship at ten o'clock of the forenoon watch.

The fresh night air was welcome and refreshing and all of them started to talk at once about the evening and their observations of the people there until Merriman stopped them. "Tomorrow, gentlemen, we'll talk it over tomorrow."

Chapter Twenty-Six

Things come to a head

The next morning Merriman called Mr Grahame and Lieutenants Laing and Andrews down to his cabin for a discussion. He started the ball rolling by saying, "I must tell you about the lucky escape I had. You may have seen Mrs Egerton and I go outside? Well she tried to seduce me, but she failed, I declined her advances. I was most embarrassed and when we came back in, I saw her give a small shake of her head to her husband. I think she hoped to find out more about our reason for being here. Did any of you find people asking you anything like that?"

"No, sir, all the women were interested in was fashions and gossip and the men wanted to know about the political affairs in London." The others said the same and they were no further forward when somebody knocked at the door.

"Come," called Merriman. "Oh, it's you, Mr Shrigley, what do you want?"

The midshipman stood nervously in front of them, cleared his throat and said, "Last night, sir, you know Mr Cuthbert and Lieutenant St James and I went ashore to find a hotel where we might get a different kind of meal. We found a nice, clean place and had a lovely meal, but it was a bit too spicy for my taste, sir."

"Yes, yes, come to the point boy, why are you here?"

"Sorry, sir. If you remember, sir, back when we were in the Irish Sea, we were stopping small trading ships looking for anything suspicious. On one ship we stopped we saw two men, one fat and the other with a face wrinkled like a walnut, Mr Andrews saw them too didn't you, sir?"

"Yes, I remember, and you said you thought they were up to no good, sir. Come on, Mr Shrigley, what else?"

"Well, sir, we were eating at a table in a sort of alcove when I saw those same two men come in for a meal."

Merriman glanced across at Andrews and said sharply, "Are you certain of this, Mr Shrigley? It could be very important. Come on, speak up."

"Ye-yes, sir, I'm sure, sir. They are very distinctive, but the biggest man had lost a lot of weight. I don't think they saw me, sir."

"Thank you, Mr Shrigley, that will be all, you may go."

"Thank you, sir, but Mr Salmon the gunner and Seaman Jackson are waiting to see you, sir. They have only just come aboard."

"Right then, send them in."

Salmon and Jackson came in cautiously, after all this was the captain's cabin and they were faced by all the senior officers of the *Aphrodite*.

"Yes, what happened to you two last night?"

"Not very much, sir," said Mr Salmon. "We watched the Jew's place in Ship Street like you said but the only three people we saw were two men, late, knocking on the door. A man opened it holding a lantern and let 'em in. We caught only a quick glimpse of the face of the smallest man, all seamed and wrinkled he was, sir. Then there was a woman, sir, she arrived separately after the others, but we couldn't see her face. She left very soon after. We waited all night and into the morning, but we saw nobody else. I 'ope that 'elps, sir."

"I believe it might, I'm sure it will. Thank you, you've both done well. My compliments to the officer of the watch and ask him to ensure that you have an extra tot of rum."

They both grinned. "Aye-aye, sir, and thank you."

When they had gone, Merriman gave a big sigh, smiled, and said, "Gentlemen, with what those two said and what Mr Shrigley said, I have my suspicion that they are the men wanted in England for treason. If I am correct, they were involved with the French agent Moreau, passing messages between him and Irish rebels. One of them is a lawyer and the other was his clerk. Now then, the question is, what do we do? We can ask the military to arrest them and anyone else they find there or wait until we can find proof of a connection they may have with the Egerton's. Think about it, gentlemen, whilst Mr Grahame and I must go to see the Admiral."

Chapter Twenty-Seven

A Murder is planned

Meanwhile Robinson and Beadle were in a panic. Beadle had seen Shrigley at an alcove table when they went for a meal but couldn't be certain that they had been recognised, but... The doubt persisted and they argued for most of the night. Should they stay and hope they had not been recognised or should they run?

Of course, that led to the argument about where they should run to. They did not have enough money to pay for a passage out even if they could find a captain to take them and their last experiences showed them that they could not trust such a man. They could steal Meyberg's two horses and disappear inland somewhere, but they didn't know the island and horrible tales of travellers being attacked, robbed, and murdered by the Maroons – the escaped slaves - very quickly put them off that idea.

They argued for hours without making a decision until one of them voiced the idea that both of them had been thinking. Robinson was the first to say it. "I think we must kill the boy. If we aren't arrested in the morning maybe he didn't recognise us or at least he hasn't told anybody yet."

"Yes, I think we must," replied Beadle. "But how? We may not see him again though if he comes ashore tomorrow we may have the opportunity." He opened a drawer and showed Robinson a pair of pistols. "These will do the job if we can get near enough, perhaps dressed roughly like men of the streets."

"Where did you get those things?" said Robinson.

Beadle tapped his nose slyly. "I stole them from one of the plantation houses I was sent to with letters. A big place it was with pistols, muskets, and swords all over the place inside, so I took a chance. I shall have to go out and get some powder and shot early in the morning, if we aren't arrested," he added as an afterthought.

In the event nothing out of the ordinary happened. Beadle bought powder and shot for his pistols and came back and loaded them.

"Now we shall have to wait near to where he might go to eat and try a shot tonight," he said. "I'd better do it, couldn't trust you to aim straight, your hands shake too much even if you can pluck up the courage," he said sneeringly.

Of course, in time, their original status of lawyer and clerk had dissolved and increasingly it was Beadle who made the decisions for the pair of them. As the day wore on and nobody came to arrest them, they began to hope but nevertheless decided to press ahead with the plan to kill the boy. In the course of one of his trips as a messenger Beadle bought some rough and ready second-hand clothing which would serve their purpose and that night they set out with murder in mind.

Chapter Twenty-Eight

Merriman makes plans

On arrival at the Admiral's offices, Merriman and Grahame were joined by Governor Sir George Scarrow and two soldiers from the previous night's party. The soldiers were introduced as Colonel Sir Henry Weatherby, a tall, languid, but keen-eyed man, and Major Duncan James, a short, stocky man by his accent a Scot. Admiral Hawkesby was there too with his Flag Captain.

The Governor opened the proceedings. "Captain Merriman, I have taken the liberty of telling these gentlemen all that we discussed yesterday in my place, including what you know about Egerton. They are both in favour of arresting all of them, unless you have a good reason not to."

"I have, sir," said Merriman. He related all that his men had discovered, the supposed recognition of the two traitors and their connection with Meyberg, and his attempted seduction by Isabella Egerton. "I am certain that she was attempting to learn why we are here."

"The lovely Isabella, Captain?" said Major James. "You lucky dog, I wouldn't mind a session with her, eh, what."

"Nothing happened, sir, and we came inside," said Merriman stiffly. "And if you are implying that I..."

He was interrupted by the Colonel. "I don't believe the Major intended anything disrespectful, sir, but she is the talk of the town and has used her wiles before on many of us."

"That is right, Captain, I hope you will accept my apology. I meant nothing personal," said the Major.

"Apology accepted, Major. I have already forgotten the matter." Merriman continued his reasoning, "Both before and after Mrs Egerton and I went out, I caught her and her husband exchanging slight signals. I think she may be as involved as her husband, but I know next to nothing about her."

"Well, I do. She is supposed to be Spanish with a lot of French blood in her and it is entirely possible she could be working for our enemies although Spain is nominally our ally, at least for the moment."

"Quite possible, sir," interjected the Admiral. "We have had trouble with Spain before and I wouldn't be surprised if they joined France to benefit from Bonaparte's conquests. But continue, Captain. Have you any more ideas?"

"Yes, sir, I have. So far, we have little more than hearsay and circumstantial evidence. I am not a lawyer, but I suspect much of it would probably not stand up in court. If I may suggest, gentlemen, the supposed recognition of the traitors from England was made by my Midshipman. I don't doubt him, but another witness would help. My Lieutenant Andrews was with him when we stopped a suspicious trading ship in the Irish Sea many months ago. They both mentioned at the time their misgivings about two of the passengers. I think that if both of them go for a meal at the same time and the same place as last night they may see them there. That and with what I know would certainly see them hanged. Sir George told me that the lawyer Meyberg is suspected of dealing in stolen goods and many other things, so if we wait until early tomorrow then we could raid the place and catch them all together and find out if there really is a connection with Egerton."

There was silence for a few minutes as they all considered what Merriman had said. The Admiral was the first to break the silence saying, "Gentlemen, I agree with Captain Merriman, we should not be too hasty, another day might give us that extra evidence and then we have two traitors mixed up with the rogue Meyberg and who knows what we might find out."

All of them nodded in agreement and the Colonel said, "I quite agree, and I would like to congratulate the Captain on his discoveries so far. It is a pleasure to know you, sir. If I may invite you to dinner in my officer's mess, I would consider it an honour, sir, if you would accept, and of course Mr Grahame as well."

"Thank you, sir, we would be delighted to accept but I would like to wait until tomorrow after the events planned have finished."

"Very good, Captain, tomorrow it is. Meanwhile I will arrange for some of my men to hold themselves ready for the morning. Major, would you arrange that? In the utmost secrecy. Don't tell the men anything yet."

With nothing further of merit to discuss, the meeting then broke up and Merriman and Grahame returned to *Aphrodite*.

Chapter Twenty-Nine

The Plans work and a Traitor is killed

Back aboard *Aphrodite,* Merriman wasted no time in calling Andrews and Shrigley to his cabin, reminding Andrews about Shrigley's report and what had been decided.

"So, I want both of you to go ashore again tonight, with Mr Gorman, and go to the hotel for a meal at the same time as last night. And go armed this time. I will have Mr St James with some of his marines nearby in case you have difficulties, and some soldiers will be available as well to surround Meyberg's place in the morning. I don't doubt your report, Mr Shrigley, but the law demands two definite witnesses. If they saw and recognised you last night they might even try to kill you. We don't know what will happen tonight but be prepared for anything and be alert. Any questions?"

The orders were clear and the three men walked slowly to the hotel that evening with Shrigley loudly proclaiming the merits of the food they would get there. They passed a group of fifteen marines hidden just out of sight in an alley and only a little further on they saw Lieutenant St James and two other marines hidden in a dark doorway only a few paces from the hotel entrance. None of the three paused but they heard the Marine Lieutenant whisper, "We've been here for half an hour and seen nothing. Good luck."

As they reached the door and stepped into the light of the lantern overhead, Andrews suddenly shouted, "Down, down."

As they bent low and scattered, a pistol shot rang out. The ball struck the stone door post just above Shrigley's head, far too close for comfort. Andrews and Gorman each had a pistol ready and fired into the area they thought the shot had come from. They saw nothing but heard a squeal from somebody either scared by a near miss or even wounded. St James and his men ran past them, and the Lieutenant shouted, "I saw where the shot came from. We'll catch him."

The two marines with fixed bayonets followed close behind him into the darkness. They heard some confused shouting and another pistol shot then the remaining marines arrived too and closed around the three officers with their weapons at the ready.

A marine Sergeant disappeared into the hotel and emerged a few moments later carrying a big lantern. "Good man," shouted Andrews. "Let's follow them."

They rounded the corner and the light revealed St James bending over a huddled body lying in the gutter.

"We found this one, but we didn't shoot him. His companion must have shot him. Bring that lantern closer, Sergeant, let's have a good look at him. Yes I thought so, one of you gentlemen hit him, here in the leg and he couldn't keep up with the other man, so he was shot again, in the belly. I'll turn him over."

Andrews and Shrigley bent over the man, saw that he was still breathing and nodded to each other before Andrews said, "Yes, we know him, he is one of the men we saw back home, and he is wanted for treason and murder. He is still alive, but not for long, I think. Here, you marines, carry him round to the front where there is more light."

They laid him on the rough cobbles near to the hotel door where he lay moaning and clutching the wound in his belly.

"Nothing we can do for him now" said Andrews, bending over him. "Who are you, what is your name and who shot you?"

The man moaned, opened his eyes, and murmured "Name is Jeremiah Robinson. I was a lawyer… an—and a g'good one. Got involved with Irish…men and a French agent named Moreau. They bl'..bl'…blackmailed me into helping them." The man rallied a bit and managed to add, "That bastard of a clerk of mine, Beadle, shot me, couldn't k' k' keep up with 'im after you shot me…" His voice faded, he clutched himself tighter, and then with a soft moan escaping his lips it was all over.

Andrews stood up and gave an order to Mr St James. "Bring all your men, except two, they can bring the body after us. The rest of you come with me and bring that lantern."

He led off at a run, following the directions given by Salmon and Jackson earlier. They brought him to the premises of the infamous Meyberg, easily identified by the newly painted sign. "Mr St James, if you would take some of your men round the back and try to stop anyone leaving."

Andrews gave them a few minutes and Salmon and Jackson appeared out of the darkness, nearly skewered on a nervous marine's bayonet. "Mr Andrews, sir, we saw the little wizened-face man come only a minute ago, but nobody let him in, so he ran off up the street, sir."

Andrews pounded on the door with the butt of his pistol, shouting, "Open up, open up in the name of the King, I demand you open up."

He shouted several times but with no result then beckoned the two biggest marines and ordered them to break down the door. They put their shoulders to the door but with no result then backed off further and tried again. This time the door gave way with a sound of splintering wood. A pistol shot sounded from inside and one of the marines fell back clutching his shoulder.

Immediately Andrews shouted, "Come out whoever you are, or I will order my marines to shoot." There was no reply so he ordered, "Marines, fire into the doorway."

They did so and there was the sound of the shot hitting wood but no sound of a man. Andrews drew his sword and said, "Marines, follow me."

They crashed inside with the sergeant carrying the lantern following but found nobody. More lanterns were found, lit, and all was revealed.

They discovered a locked door to the side, a stairway leading above and a passage to a back door and a partly open door ahead of them. The Sergeant sent three marines upstairs and then Andrews approached the door.

"Keep to the side, you men," he said, and he reached out from the side of the door and gently pushed it open with his sword. This revealed the body of a big, fat man slumped over a desk in the middle of the room with a pistol in his hand. He was quite dead with a pool of blood spreading out onto some papers and the desktop.

Andrews pushed him to the floor, sheathing his sword with a sigh of relief just as a pounding was heard on the back door and St James shouting, "We're coming in, Mr Andrews. Don't shoot."

"It's alright, you can come in," replied Andrews just as one of the marines sent upstairs came down and reported that they had found nobody and two doors locked.

"Plenty of papers and books up there, sir, but I can't read them."

"Right then, stay up there until I come. Ah, Edward, the party's over, did you find or see anything out there?"

"No, David, but just as we got here a man on a horse burst out of the yard at the back and disappeared before we could shoot. There is another horse there in a stable and some dirty sheds but without lights I don't know what is in them."

"Right, I suggest two of your men take a lantern and see what they can find. As you can see there are a lot of books and papers here and more of the same upstairs. If we can find some bags and sacks we should take everything back to the Governor's office. There is a locked room near the front door, have it and others upstairs opened, and we'll see what we can find. Mr Gorman can go with you."

"Aye-aye, Sir," said St James. He motioned to three marines standing by and they all disappeared into the passage.

Andrews borrowed a marine's bayonet and tried to open the locked drawers without success.

"Here, sir, let me, I've opened plenty before I joined the Jollies," said the marine as he easily broke into the desk, leaving the drawers open.

The event reminded Andrews what an eclectic mix of men could be found in the navy, their past forgotten. "Good man, what's your name?"

"Jones Two, sir," said the man standing stiffly to attention.

"Well done, Jones Two, now go and help where you can. I want sacks or boxes or sheets to carry all these papers."

The man disappeared with a quick "Aye-aye, sir" just as St James came in with a big smile on his face.

"There are two rooms stuffed full of rolls of silk, satin and boxes of leather goods, some jewellery and crates of rum and brandy. I've put the Sergeant in charge upstairs and a reliable corporal on guard downstairs. No normal place would have such a mixture and I think it may all be stolen."

Eventually all was done and the papers and documents were bundled into sacks and boxes, but Andrews put all the contents of the desk in a separate bag and kept it with him. They left, leaving the Sergeant, the Corporal and six marines to guard the place. The two bodies were left in the back yard.

Chapter Thirty

The End of another Traitor

Meanwhile Meyberg was riding as fast as he could to a plantation where he hoped to find a place to hide. His horse stumbled in the darkness and fell, breaking its neck, trapping Meyberg's leg beneath its body and, try though he might to escape, he was held firmly. Daylight was beginning to steal over the sky when a running man approached him.

"Help me, please help me," he called.

The man stopped and moved closer until Meyberg recognised him. It was Beadle, panting for breath.

"What are you doing here?" gasped Meyberg, grimacing in pain.

"Same as you I expect, trying to escape, your office was raided and I only just managed to get away," said Beadle. "I was going to go to the plantation you sent me to with your letters. I know you weren't an honest man so I thought I could hide there. Oh, and Robinson is dead, they caught him."

"That's where I was going until this wretched nag fell on me. If you can help me, we could go on together. They know me there and I can speak for you."

After much struggling and heaving Meyberg's leg was freed and they set off together, slowly because Meyberg had a severe limp.

At the Egerton plantation it was a scene of feverish activity, slaves were loading furniture and bundles of goods onto mule-drawn wagons and Egerton and his wife were chivvying them on. A smaller carriage was loaded with various boxes, clothing, and weapons whilst Isabelle was there screaming at the slaves to work faster. She saw Beadle and Meyberg as they approached and called to her husband.

He turned and asked them, "What are you two doing here? We are leaving and there's no room for you."

"Please, sir, I've served you well for many years and my friend too, can't we come with you?" begged Meyberg.

"No, and that is final. I already knew that your place was raided. God does not know what will be found there to tell people what we do, nor can I leave you here to talk if captured."

He called two rough-looking men to him and said, "Take these two away; I don't want to see them again."

He drew his hand across his throat significantly as the men grabbed Meyberg and Beadle and started to drag them towards some trees.

"Where are you taking us?" screamed Beadle. "I can help you."

"Shut your mouth. You'll soon see," snarled one of the roughs.

Meyberg, limping painfully, offered no resistance. He seemed to have accepted his fate and said quietly, "They're going to kill us you fool, it's obvious."

"No," screamed Beadle, struggling like a mad thing. "You can't, you can't."

The men took no notice and dragged them both behind the trees and threw them to the ground. A few moments later Egerton heard two pistol shots and the two men reappeared, one of them casually wiping his knife on a handful of grass.

"That will have to do," shouted Egerton to the slaves. "We have to go."

He and his wife climbed into the carriage and set off down a different road followed by the lumbering wagons.

Chapter Thirty-One

Documents and more Documents

While his men were ashore, Merriman was in a fever of impatience to know what had happened. He had implicit trust in his officers but knew something unexpected could always happen. He paced his cabin until the low headroom made it too uncomfortable and he was forced on deck. There, he walked up and down until he realised that his image of the calm and confident Master and Commander, a respected Captain of the Royal Navy was in danger of being lost. He was standing looking ashore when Mr Grahame appeared beside him. Only the duty watch were on deck and they were pretending not to notice him, but they might wonder.

Merriman turned to him saying, "A lovely night, sir, mild up here but my cabin's too hot..."

He was interrupted by the faint sound of shots and a little later the muffled sound of a volley of musketry.

"Lieutenant Laing,' Merriman called, "my gig, with the crew armed. I must see what is going on."

Laing bellowed orders and Merriman's boat crew arrived on deck, some of them still pulling on their shirts. The boat, tied up astern, was quickly pulled alongside and with the bos'n Owen bawling orders the crew practically fell in followed more slowly by Merriman with all the dignity he could muster.

The boat practically flew over the water and pulled up alongside some weed-covered stone steps. "Three of you come with me, the rest of you stay here," Merriman said.

On the quayside he paused with three armed men behind him. One of them was Owen who silently handed him his sword. Hardly had they moved from the quayside then the main party of marines and seamen appeared burdened with sacks, boxes and sheets tied up round something. Lieutenants Andrews and St

John led them, carrying lanterns and stopped so abruptly that the men behind bumped into one another and some bundles fell onto the cobbles.

Andrews touched his hat and reported. "Sir, the plan almost succeeded, but we were shot at. No harm done, we fired back and got one of them. He died but told us he was a lawyer name of Johnson. The other man fled but we raided the man Meyberg's place, but he also fled before we could stop him."

"Have we any casualties, Mr Andrews?" asked Merriman.

"Only one, sir, a marine with a pistol ball in his shoulder. We brought all the papers and records and accounting books we could find," he said, indicating the load carried by the sweating marines and seamen. "We left a guard on the place, sir, because we found a lot of expensive goods there."

"Well done, you men, take a rest. Owen, take the gig back with the wounded marine and fetch the cutter to carry us all and these bundles back to the ship."

While they waited, the officers related more of what had happened. "I broke into a big desk, at least marine Jones Two did, and I put everything in it into a separate bundle. Might be the most important of the lot, sir," said Andrews.

"It may be so, but with everything back on board we can investigate it all in the morning. I see some soldiers coming to find out what is happening, I'll deal with them now and they can report back to their officers."

On board *Aphrodite,* the bundles were put in various secure places and the men dismissed. Mr Grahame was all agog to know what had happened and once in Merriman's cabin he was given a brief account.

"All sounds very successful, James, but as you say we can look at these books and papers in daylight tomorrow."

Chapter Thirty-Two

Important Information Found

Aboard *Aphrodite,* Merriman and Grahame with Andrews and St John were spreading papers and books all over the cabin sole which was covered by a black and white checkered canvas.

St James knelt over a pile of account books but, said, "Only records of financial dealings with the names of his customers, sir. Perhaps the Governor's secretary can sort out the names. There's another book here listing all the people he has lent money to, but it all seems innocuous, sir."

"Right, there is nothing much here in all these papers either," said Merriman. "Let us pile all of them in that corner and we can concentrate on the items David took from Meyberg's locked desk."

The contents of the desk revealed a lot. Most of the documents concerned dealings with Egerton, goods bought and sold and copies of incriminating letters between the two men. There was no doubt that Egerton was the man they were after, and they sat back in satisfaction.

"We've got him, James," said Grahame.

Merriman shook his head and replied, "We have the proof, but we haven't got the man, sir."

They sat in silence for some minutes, thinking before Merriman shot to his feet saying, "Egerton must have been warned by now and will want to escape. Are any of the ships in the harbour his?"

"Yes, there are three I think," said Andrews scrabbling about among the papers. "Here we are, a large trading vessel called the *Enterprise* and two of his own fleet of small warships are here. I've seen them, the trader is more like an East Indiaman and probably pierced for cannon, and the other two are

Adventure and *Avenger*. I've seen them, sir, all together on the other side of the harbour."

"Good," said Merriman. "I shall go and tell the Admiral what we have found, and you, Mr Andrews, can go and see the Colonel with my compliments. Tell him everything and ask will he set a guard on Meyberg's house to let our marines come back here. Mr Grahame, would you go and see Sir George and take all those papers and documents to him? Tell him about the stolen goods, he will have to deal with them. I'll detail a petty officer and some men to carry all this stuff to the boat and up to the Governor's offices for you. And would you take your uncle ashore with you as I think there will be some fighting to be done? Any questions, gentlemen? No? Then let us begin."

Very quickly the cutter delivered them and the bundles further along the quayside and each set off to see the various people as Merriman had ordered. Aboard the Flagship he was immediately shown in to see the Admiral who listened keenly to all he was told.

"It seems you have done well, Mr Merriman. Do you think Egerton will try to escape by sea in his own ship?"

"I'm certain of it, sir, he has nowhere else here he can go. The papers and books we found incriminate him without a shadow of a doubt so what else can he do? And he has three ships here now on the other side of the harbour."

"Has he, by Jove? Can you see them from here?"

"From the deck, sir, but not from your cabin."

They both went on deck and surveyed the ships by telescope. The trader was seen to be loading and all three seemed to be preparing to sail.

The Admiral was not slow to make up his mind. "If they get too far away, we shall lose them. You will take your ship and stop them or at least follow them and I'll give the captains of our two frigates orders to follow you as rapidly as they can. Now be off with you."

Chapter Thirty-Three

The chase is on

As he was rowed back to his ship, Merriman could see the signal flags fluttering on the Flagship and almost immediately boats left the two frigates taking the two Captains to the Admiral. He realised also that men were almost running aloft on both and looking back at the signal flags he saw the command 'Prepare to sail' flying.

He arrived back to his own ship just as the cutter bearing his officers and the marines did. They backed water to allow him on board first with the bos'n's whistles loud and a depleted marine guard standing there under command of a corporal and the First Lieutenant waiting to greet him.

"Mr Laing, we must leave at once, all hands prepare for leaving harbour."

Laing bellowed orders and it was all bustle, the anchor party mustered on the fo'c'sle, groups of men gathering below each mast to be checked off by their petty officers before hastening aloft and out onto the yards. Others hauled the boats alongside to be lifted into their places on deck and yet more men manning the capstan to raise the anchor.

Merriman smiled in satisfaction. All appeared to be chaos, but he knew that everybody knew his place and order was soon restored with everybody looking towards him for orders. He looked round, saw Lieutenant Andrews but not Mr Grahame, so asked, "Mr Andrews, where is Mr Grahame?"

"He told me to go without him, sir, said it would take hours before all the papers were sorted by himself and the Governor's secretaries and clerks."

"We'll have to leave him then."

Merriman turned to Lieutenant Laing and nodded. It was all Laing needed, he shouted the order to the waiting men, and then everything happened at once.

The men at the windlass began to bring the ship up to her anchor and other men started hoisting the headsails. As soon as the anchor cable was up and down, indicating that the anchor was clear, the officer there, Lieutenant Gorman, signalled back to the quarter deck where Laing bellowed the order, "Haul in fores'l sheets, quickly now you lazy fools." Indeed, as the anchor ceased to grip, the ship's head began to turn the wrong way and it was only the speedy action with the jib sheets that swung it back to be sheeted in on the other tack.

"Tops'ls now, Mr Laing," said Merriman.

At the order, the Topmen already aloft loosed the gaskets and, as the sail was quickly sheeted home, *Aphrodite* slowly headed for the harbour entrance.

Chapter Thirty-Four

The Chase and Death at Sea

"Egerton's ships are away, sir," reported the Master. "They must have started as soon as the Admiral's signals were hoisted. They will beat us out to the open sea."

It was even so; the big Indiaman was away ahead of the two smaller ships.

"Thank you, Mr Cuthbert, I can see that. They left wagons full of stuff on the quayside, so they were in great haste to get away. Now, Master, I'll have all the sail she will carry, including the stuns'ls. We have to catch those ships."

Aphrodite was one of the new breed of sloops with three masts instead of the more usual two and flush decked. The fore and main masts were rigged with large square sails and the mizzen mast with fore and aft sails. She was really a small version of a frigate with a single row of gun ports hiding her armament. She was well coppered below and when Merriman first saw her the previous year, he had said "By God, she'll be a flyer this one", and a flyer she certainly was. The wind was on her starboard quarter as they left harbour, but it gradually veered forward to blow from just abaft the main mast on her starboard side, the ship's best point of sailing.

Looking aft, Merriman could see the two frigates setting more sail and, being fast ships, should soon catch up. Nevertheless, *Aphrodite* was gaining on the three ships ahead, slowly but appreciably as Merriman ordered the ship to quarters for action with all guns loaded and run out. Again, there was a scene of controlled chaos as partitions were dismantled, furniture and sea chests taken below, the chests put together in the orlop to form a rough operating table for the surgeon's grisly work.

The gun crews closed up and the little powder monkeys appeared from below with the first charges for the guns. The sound of the marine drummer boy's repetitive tattoo never failed to stir Merriman and he walked up and down his small quarterdeck with almost a smile on his face.

Mr Cuthbert, the elderly master, was busy streaming the log and taking sights of the frigates behind and the ships in front. "I've never seen this ship move so fast before, sir. She's catching up and the frigates are only reducing our lead very slowly."

Merriman beckoned the First Lieutenant and the Marine Lieutenant St James to join him with the Master near the big ship's wheel. "Now, gentlemen this is what I propose to do if this wind holds. We shall be up with that small sloop within perhaps fifteen minutes, a full broadside as we pass and then I'll leave her for a frigate whilst we press on. I want to pass the corvette as soon as I can. The Indiaman is the one we must stop. When we reach the corvette I'll have Mr Salmon put a few shots into her stern to try and damage her rudder, but I don't want to pass too close to it, and as we do, only one or two broadsides, Mr Laing, if you please. And have the stuns'ls and courses off as soon as we get closer but be ready to set them again as soon as we are past."

"Aye-aye, sir," both repeated before Cuthbert went back to his post by the wheel and Laing summoned all the warrant officers concerned to tell them what the orders were and what they had to do. In the event the small sloop veered away as *Aphrodite* approached and turned towards the coast in a bid to escape the expected gunfire.

"Mr Laing," shouted Merriman, "don't waste a full broadside on that one. Six cannon will be enough as they bear."

"Aye-aye, sir," Laing replied and passed the order to Lieutenant Gorman at his station in command of the larboard battery.

Gorman in turn passed the order to his gun captains and as *Aphrodite* passed the sloop the six guns fired almost together. Splashes showed where four of them missed but two hit the stern with no apparent damage apart from a shower of splinters.

Merriman walked forward to the two big twenty five pounder bowchasers on the fo'c'sle where Midshipman Oakley was in command. He said to Oakley and the two gun captains, "As soon as that next ship is in range, open fire. I will slow down as we approach to give you more time, but I want to see at least three shots from each of you if not more, but don't rush, be sure of your aim and try to hit her rudder."

Back to the quarterdeck he went, confident that the experienced men wouldn't let Oakley make a mess of it.

Hardly had he reached the quarterdeck when the two cannons fired almost as one. One ball splashed into the sea astern of the corvette and the other, perhaps due to a slightly bigger powder charge, fell close alongside, good shooting for the first ranging shot. The months of training were bearing fruit as the crews had both guns ready to shoot again in only minutes. They fired again, but not together as before as each captain carefully judged his own time to shoot. There was no big sea running and the ship was very steady making an ideal gun platform. This time both shots hit the corvette, one smashing into the stern just above her name, *Adventure,* and the other made a hole in the aft sail.

"Reduce sail, Mr Laing."

With the main course reefed and the topsails also reefed, the ship slowed down as the corvette replied by running up her colours: the French flag. That raised a series of jeers and catcalls from *Aphrodite's* crew as Merriman gestured to Midshipman Shrigley. The boy was ready and instantly the ensign was hauled aloft.

"I'm glad to see their flag, Mr Cuthbert. Makes this a real fight as we are at war with France after all," said Merriman. "They can't claim to be American privateers."

The bowchasers spoke again for the third time, this time both together and both the balls hit, one bringing the mizzen gaff down with a crash and the other smashed into the stern.

"Bear well away from her, Mr Cuthbert, and have all the reefs shaken out. Mr Laing, a full broadside as we pass if you please."

As *Aphrodite* passed the corvette, both ships opened fire. They were fairly evenly matched in terms of size and of number of guns, but Merriman knew that the men at each of his guns would get two shots away to one of the French. The ship became a bedlam of smashing wood, lethal splinters flying across the deck and bringing men down to lie on the deck, some screaming and writhing in agony and some just lying there dead.

Another broadside ripped into the corvette before a reply came, only perhaps less than half of her guns this time. Then as *Aphrodite* passed clear, the gun smoke cleared and the full extent of the damage was seen. The corvette's main topmast was down and in falling it had tangled with the foremast. Shattered holes along the gundeck showed overturned guns and bodies everywhere with trails of blood and gore running out of the scuppers. She was finished as a fighting ship and Merriman left her to the frigates which had managed to come nearer.

Merriman thanked his stars that he had insisted on gunnery practice every day although men hated him for it. The result of that training was only too obvious. He strode to the quarterdeck rail and surveyed the damage to his own ship. The dead, only four as yet, were lying amidships and the wounded taken below to the care of Doctor McBride. Little damage could be seen aloft, and men were already aloft to repair broken ropes and lower down a torn tops'l. On deck the damage was more obvious with two cannons dismounted from smashed carriages and holes in the bulwarks. As he stood there some unknown voice yelled, "A cheer lads, a cheer for our Jimmy, and another one."

He smiled and raised his hat but shouted, "There's another one yet men but she won't have as many guns."

Aphrodite was now rapidly overhauling the Indiaman and Merriman could see her name on the transom: *Enterprise*. He determined his next move.

"Mr Laing, we'll board her. Mr Laing?"

"He is below, sir, a splinter wound in his leg, but Mr McBride says it's not too serious," reported Andrews standing behind him.

"Very well, Mr Andrews, pass the word, one broadside of chain-shot to try and dismast her and then we'll board, so have the boarding parties mustered ready. You can lead from for'ard, and I will go from aft. Oh, and make sure that our carronade gives a good account of itself before we board."

"Aye-aye, sir," replied Andrews with a big grin on his face.

Merriman turned to look aft. One frigate was alongside the corvette, but no firing could be heard. A large column of smoke could be seen further away, and the second frigate was not far astern of *Aphrodite*. Looking for'ard he could clearly see men aboard the Indiaman throwing stuff overboard in an attempt to lighten the ship. *They realise that we will catch them, and they must realise that they stand no chance against our guns. Do you no good, we've got you now* said Merriman to himself.

He raised his arms as his cox'n Owen buckled his sword about his waist. But it became clear that he was wrong. Men could be seen gathering on deck, armed men, obviously determined to fight back if their ship was boarded.

Using a speaking trumpet, Merriman shouted, "Heave to or I will fire into you."

There was no reply, but defiant shouts could be heard and the ship began to bear away to larboard.

"He's not going to surrender, sir," said Andrews.

"No, he's not. Mr Cuthbert, bring us up alongside, not too close and then we'll give her a broadside before we board. Mr Laing, what are you doing here, you're wounded?"

Laing had come back on deck, pale faced and with a bloody bandage round his thigh. "Couldn't stay away, sir, I won't be of much use if you board her, but I can still keep an eye on things from here," he said and clutched the pinrail to help keep the weight off his leg.

"Thank you, Mr Laing, we are about to open fire." Merriman shouted the order, "Fire as your guns bear."

Mr Cuthbert had already ordered the courses furled which reduced the ship's speed as she drew alongside. The broadside rippled out in a continuous roar as each gun came to bear. The damage to the Indiaman was immediately obvious, sails were shredded, some standing and running rigging was in shreds, and the carronade had loosed a devastating hail of musket balls into the men on deck.

The Master at the wheel with his Mates brought *Aphrodite* close alongside and the two ships met with a thud as the carronade released another lethal hail of balls into the men on the Indiaman's deck.

"Boarders away," yelled Merriman, leaping across the gap between the ships with his eager boarding party while others of his men threw grapnels to hold the ships together.

As Merriman landed on the deck, his foot slipped in a pool of blood and he nearly fell. A seaman ran at him with a boarding pike and would have spitted him but for Owen close behind him who deflected the pike thrust and opened up the man's throat with a vicious slash with his cutlass. Then they were in the thick of it, and it was all slash, cut and parry, tripping over wounded and dead men and parts of men whilst his men followed and spread out on either side of him. They were surrounded by screaming, swearing, sweating men, desperate to kill them.

As Merriman fought savagely but coolly he became aware that most of his enemies were shouting in English. He realised that there must be a lot of English deserters in the crew who would know the fate waiting for them if captured. Other men were shouting in French and Merriman's momentary attention on that was nearly the end of him as a Frenchman aimed a vicious slash to his head. He managed to deflect the blow but received a cut to his sword arm which slowed his riposte.

At the same time a red-coated arm with a sword thrust between them and St James panted, "Just in time, sir. He nearly had you, excuse me."

St James was a master swordsman and quickly dealt with the man with a rapid thrust to the man's throat. He fell with blood pouring from his mouth and then Merriman returned the favour by parrying a slash to the marine's side and dispatching the attacker with a thrust between his ribs.

Suddenly he heard Lieutenant Andrew's voice and his men cheering as the two groups of men met. "Nearly done, sir. They were an ill disciplined lot, no idea how to fight together, so we had to kill most of them to stop them."

The fighting was almost over, only two or three small groups of men still resisted but they were soon finished.

"Oh, I say, sir, you are wounded."

Blood was running down Merriman's arm and dripping onto the already blood-soaked deck.

"Not seriously though, David, only a slight cut, but I expect our instructor will have a few words to say," he said, referring to the regular instructional lessons given by St James.

"I haven't seen Egerton or his wife yet, have any of you?" asked Merriman as he looked around.

"I haven't seen a woman and as for the man, I don't know, sir," replied St James, pointing to the heaps of bodies lying about them. "Perhaps he is dead and she might be in a cabin."

"We must find her," said Merriman. "David, you can take charge here. Edward and I with two or three marines will go below."

The companionway led down to a short passage with two doors on either side, all open, but at a gesture from St James the marines investigated. "Nowt in 'em, sir," reported one of them in a broad Cornish accent.

"That just leaves the big cabin then. Allow me to go first with my men."

St James pushed the door open with his sword to reveal Egerton and his wife standing behind a wide table. Egerton held a pistol in front of him and his wife held a long knife. Two of the marines and Merriman followed St James, the marines holding their bayonetted muskets threateningly towards the couple.

"Ah, Captain Merriman, good to see you again, I must try and explain this little misunderstanding," said Edgerton.

"Not until you put that pistol down and you, lady, put that knife down," said Merriman sternly.

Neither of them made any move to do so and Egerton continued, "You will wonder why we are involved in buying cheap land and stolen goods. My wife as you know can be very persuasive and it was all her idea. We were wealthy, but she wanted more you s…"

He stopped as his wife turned and stabbed him screaming, "Lies, lies. I had to do what my husband ordered."

"No, it's all true, gentlemen. She persuaded me, but her father Don Carlos started it all," said Edgerton and, slowly lifting his pistol, he shot her.

The force of the ball flung her back to the cabin wall where she slowly slid down leaving a trail of blood on the panelling.

"Die, you bitch" said Egerton as he too slid to the deck.

They turned to leave but stopped as they heard a gasp from behind them. Egerton's bloody hand could be seen clinging to the edge of the table as he tried to pull himself upright, but he fell back with a groan.

St James moved round the table to see and said, "Fellow's still alive, sir, but not for long, I think."

Merriman looked at the dying man and said, "So, Le Seigneur, we ran you to earth at last."

Egerton looked up and said, "I'm not Le Seigneur, damn it." He coughed and blood filled his mouth and ran down his cheeks. He swallowed and gasped, "That's my wife's father, he was behind all of this, he... he's Span... Spanish, and you'll never find him." Those were the last words he ever spoke; he convulsed, coughed, and died.

"My God, I didn't expect this, sir," said St James as they all stood staring.

"No, neither did I, but we can't do anything for them for now."

As they left the cabin, a seaman came hurriedly down the companion ladder, saw Merriman, knuckled his forehead, and gasped, "Frigate's 'ere, sir. Captain's coming over."

The frigate captain climbed aboard to such ceremony as Merriman could muster with his marines and one lone bos'n's whistle, and as he did so he looked about him at the dead and wounded littering the deck. Merriman stepped forward and touched his forehead in welcome, his hat had disappeared.

"Welcome aboard, sir. I apologise for the poor welcome but..."

The captain waved his hand dismissively. "I'm Langworthy and don't worry about that, Captain. I see you have done well. The Admiral will be pleased. Have you captured the man Egerton?"

"Yes and no, sir. He and his wife are below, they killed each other."

"A pity, Captain, the Admiral was hoping for a public trial and a hanging. But I suppose we should have expected something like that to happen. Now we must return to Kingston with the prizes and prisoners. Have you enough fit men to form a prize crew, or shall I send some over?"

"Thank you, sir, that would be appreciated. I don't yet know how many men I have lost, but this ship will need a lot of work aloft before going very far."

"So, I see. Anyway let me know what you want, I'll stand nearby."

And so, after much repair to the Indiaman's rigging and new sails brought up from her sail room, they proceeded towards Kingston. The dead were disposed of over the side and the prisoners securely locked below divided between all the ships.

Chapter Thirty-Five

Reports and legal difficulties

After the routine gun salutes between the ships and the Flag, the three naval ships and the prize corvette all anchored in the harbour. The captured ship *Enterprise* was taken alongside the wharf she had left only hours before. In response to flag signals, Merriman and the captains of the two frigates hastily had themselves rowed over to the Flagship.

They climbed aboard one after the other to the expected ceremony. Not often did three captains arrive so closely together and the marines who fired the first salute had to have their places taken by more marines and so on. They were greeted by the Flag Captain who led them below to where Admiral Hawkesby was waiting, surprisingly accompanied by Governor Scarrow and Mr Grahame.

"Come in, gentlemen, come in and seat yourselves. I see you have been successful with two prizes out of the three you chased."

A servant appeared with a tray of glasses and began to serve various drinks from a row of bottles on a sideboard. When all were served the Admiral raised his glass and said, "Your health, gentlemen. And now Captain Wykeham, will you start please?"

Wykeham, the senior of the two frigate captains, then related all that had happened until he caught up with the *Aphrodite*. He turned to Merriman, "Damnably fast ship you have, Captain. I wouldn't have caught up with you had you not shortened sail to fire into the corvette and then stopped to engage the *Enterprise*. Admiral, with your permission I will ask Captain Merriman to continue from here."

Hawkesby nodded and Merriman began, "Thank you, sir, yes my ship is fast and with the advantage of that speed I overhauled the *Enterprise* and asked them to surrender. They took no notice, so I fired a broadside and then we boarded her. The crew was a mixture of French, Spanish and English, sir, who knew what fate would await them if they surrendered so they fought hard but to no avail. My Marine Lieutenant St James and some marines found Mr Egerton and his wife below and called me. It seemed that he wanted to talk his way out of it by blaming his wife for all he had done. She blamed him and stabbed him and then he shot her. They are both dead now, sir. I had lost several men, but Captain Wykeham sent some of his men over to help my prize crew and, well, here we are, sir."

"Excellent report, gentlemen," said the Admiral. "But what happened to the smaller sloop?"

"That too was taken, thanks to Captain Merriman," said Wykeham. "His shots hit her stern and damaged her steering. Captain Parsons, would you continue?" "

Yes, sir. Well, she ran aground, and her crew swam ashore. We couldn't get closer because of the shallow water so they managed to escape. I sent my First Lieutenant and the marines to take the ship but thank goodness they hadn't reached her before she blew up. A total loss, sir. She burned to the waterline."

"A very successful enterprise, gentlemen," said the Admiral. "Governor, have you anything to add?"

"Only to congratulate these officers, Admiral. Thanks to them an evil core has been removed from our society. Captain Merriman, the documents you captured have proved to be invaluable, but it could take lawyers months to sort it all out and try and return some of the stolen goods to the rightful owners, even if it is possible. Beside the silks and other items found at Isaac Meyberg's premises, some of the carts they left on the quayside are full of more goods, coffee, brandy, tobacco, and wine which we can only assume to be stolen. I sent soldiers to Egerton's plantation where they found more of the same. And of course, there is whatever may be found on that ship you captured."

He paused and then said, "I don't suppose we shall ever find the original owners as the documents don't tell us where all that came from. All privateer loot I shouldn't wonder and what cannot be claimed will have to be sold, and the ships you caught will be sold. Maybe the corvette could be of use to the navy, Admiral?"

"Yes, Sir George, maybe but it will have to be surveyed first. And now, gentlemen, I urge you all to have another drink. Business is over and I want to hear more about your racehorse of a ship, Captain Merriman, as I'm sure you other gentlemen do."

The officers immediately started asking questions all at once, about the ship's design, her speed, her rig, and her armament. Merriman held up his arms in surrender.

"Gentlemen, gentlemen, enough, I'll try and answer you all together. First, she is one of the first of a new breed of sloop with slim lines for'ard and a deep keel. As you know she is fitted with square sails on two of the three masts plus the usual jibs and trysails and I am constantly surprised and delighted at how fast she is and how close to the wind she will sail. The deep keel means of course that she can beat to windward without a great deal of rolling. My crew is as you would expect, and my guns are nine-pounders."

"There's more though isn't there, Captain," asked Wykeham. "You have two big bow chasers and two smashers on the foredeck, a heavy armament for a sloop and you have marines as well, and that isn't usual either, is it?"

"No, sir, it isn't. When I took over command she was fitted out as you see her and with the marines. That was because the Admiralty wanted the ship for a special mission in the Irish Sea with Mr Grahame. I don't really know what or how much I should tell you about that. Perhaps Mr Grahame would tell you, after all I am nominally under his command. Mr Grahame?"

"All I will say, gentlemen, is that we were after French spies and smugglers and other miscellaneous traitors and thieves, all banded together in a plot to capture the Lord Lieutenant of Ireland. It failed miserably thanks to Captain Merriman whose sterling work saved the lives of the Lord Lieutenant and my own."

"By God, sir, I wish you Mr Merriman and your ship were part of my command. We need more of such ships and men. Is the Admiralty building more do you know?"

"I believe so, sir, but how many I can't say," replied Merriman who was becoming restless under the gaze of his superiors.

He was saved from more talk of ships by Captain Wykeham asking, "Captain, your name is not a common one and I am minded of another Captain Merriman, and a fine captain he was. I had the honour of serving under him as a very junior midshipman aboard the frigate *Alexis*. Are you related by any chance?"

"Indeed I am, sir. He is my father and many tales he told me of his time at sea and of the *Alexis*. He retired to the country in Cheshire with my mother and I am his first born. He has a daughter and another son too."

"I'm pleased he survived. Led us into many hair-raising adventures, he did. I'd be obliged if you will remind him of his little Midshipman Wykeham when you next see him."

"That I will do, sir. He will be delighted to hear from you."

On that note, the meeting dissolved with the Governor inviting them all to dinner the next day. The captains departed to their own ships to write up their various reports in full for the Admiral. Of course, Grahame went back with Merriman.

Chapter Thirty-Six

Repairs and preparations for Departure

Back aboard, Merriman lost no time before asking for reports on the condition of his ship. Mr Laing met him, all smiles although limping about on a stick. He reported that most of the repairs had already been completed.

"The carpenter and his mates have repaired the two damaged gun carriages. The guns will be swayed up shortly, sir. All the damaged ropes aloft have been repaired and he reports no damage to the hull except for the bulwarks on the larboard side which as you can see are being repaired as we speak. He estimates all repairs will be completed in two or three hours. Oh yes, sir, he requests permission to go ashore to the dockyard to obtain some new timber."

"He's a good man, our carpenter, he'll only ask if he needs it. Have him make a list and I'll sign it. See to it if you please, Colin, and then sit down and take the weight off your leg."

"Yes, sir. I've also arranged for fresh water and supplies of fresh food, all that will be aboard shortly. I think that's all, sir."

Below, Merriman found Grahame seated with his head in his hands and with his uncle there with him. "Too much brandy, James, too much brandy. I don't usually drink so much but it was hard not to with all that was going on. Wine I can take but brandy, no."

"Don't worry, sir, my head feels a bit the same but some of Peters' coffee will soon make us feel better. Peters, coffee, and hurry about it," Merriman shouted.

Peters instantly appeared with a jug of coffee and three mugs. "Knew you would want this, sir. Brewed it as soon as you came aboard and I've been keeping it warm," he said in an aggrieved tone of voice.

"Thank you, Peters, I should have known. I apologise for shouting at you."

Peters smiled a little, poured out the coffee, set down the jug and left the cabin. The men drank the coffee in silence, busy with their own thoughts for a while before Merriman said, "I didn't say so when we were with the Admiral and the others, but Egerton wasn't the one they called 'Le Seigneur'. Before he died, he said it was his wife's father, a Spaniard."

"That is a surprise, James, a real surprise. That means we have to find him if we can but that could be very difficult. If he really is a Spaniard he's probably somewhere in Hispaniola. The Spanish and French have been squabbling over it for years and there is trouble with slave risings too. Also, he could have escaped to any of the Spanish possessions in South America. With the present state of affairs at home and the fear that Spain will ally itself with France, we can't do anything that might make the political situation worse. I'll have to think on it some more," said Grahame.

Merriman asked, "Where do you think we might go next, sir, or do we stay here while the Governor and the lawyers sort things out?"

"I don't know yet, but we are to go to the Governor's dinner tomorrow and perhaps we will hear then. Now I must get my head down and my feet up, James."

The following evening, after a pleasant and enjoyable dinner, the ladies retired and left the men to their brandy and cigars. The guests were all either naval or army officers and the Governor wasted no time in sending the servants out.

"Now then, gentlemen, to business. You told us, Mr Merriman, that one of the dead men left at Meyberg's office had been a lawyer and his clerk was a small man with a heavily wrinkled face. Colonel Weatherby tells me that when the army had a really good look around Egerton's plantation, apart from all the silks, satins, brandy and such, they found two dead men. One was Meyberg and the other was the small man with the wrinkled face. Both had been shot and their throats cut. Evidently Egerton wanted to leave no traces behind him."

"Both of our traitors are accounted for it seems. We don't have to worry about them anymore, sir," said Merriman.

"No, we don't," said Grahame, "but it seems that we didn't catch the main conspirator in this cheap land purchase plot. Egerton told us just before he died that his wife's father, a Spaniard, was behind it all, but they all must have been involved in the privateering and theft, so I don't suppose that this business is completely finished yet."

Sir George commented, "You are probably right, sir. It would be too much to expect. However, my staff and I, with the Colonel and Major James have arranged for all the property that has been found to be moved into a big warehouse with an armed guard. It is staggering, absolutely staggering. A rough assessment gives us a total value of not less than seventy thousand pounds, not including the two ships. Of course, we shall have to advertise this and ask traders who have lost these goods to come forward and identify them, although I imagine many of them are dead, lost with their ships. This will take months or more but eventually what is left will be sold at public auction. If the navy buys the corvette that value is prize money to be shared out between your ships in the usual way as will the money from the sale of the *Enterprise*. The rest of the money will be put to good use here on public works."

All the captains sat there amazed until Admiral Hawkesby remarked, "Well, that will all go into the appropriate prize funds, gentlemen, and I believe a similar amount will go to the army here."

"It will, Admiral, it will. I think that is all, gentlemen. Shall we join the ladies?"

Several days passed and Merriman kept his crew busy on the multiplicity of tasks needed to keep the ship in first class fighting trim. The Governor had sent each ship a modest purse of money for the captains to share out with their men and so Merriman sent small parties of men ashore, but with only a small amount of money so that they couldn't drink themselves senseless, a common habit of sailors.

The captains of the two frigates both asked for permission to visit *Aphrodite* to see for themselves and in detail, how the ship was designed and rigged. Eventually the day came when Grahame announced that it was time he and Merriman went to see the Governor and the Admiral. Grahame explained that he felt it necessary to go back to Anguilla, Antigua, and Barbados, first of all to inform the Governors and Officers in Command all that had happened in Jamaica and also to find out if there was any more news about French activities there.

Chapter Thirty-Seven

To Anguilla and Antigua

Early one morning, with the sun just beginning to show itself above the horizon, *Aphrodite* left Kingston behind and set off for Anguilla. The wind was fair and cool, but Merriman knew that before an hour or two had passed they would all be glad to keep to the shade.

Mr Cuthbert gave a prodigious sniff and said, "I'm glad to leave that place behind, sir. Too hot for me. My charts are now fully up to date thanks to the masters of the other ships and charts I found in the cabin aboard the *Enterprise.* They gave us much more information about the waters round these islands than our Admiralty charts did."

"I'm not sorry to leave either, Master. I would have liked to go up one of the mountains to see the view, but I was advised against it. Too many bandits I'm told, escaped slaves and the like."

"Yes, sir," said the First Lieutenant who had joined them. "It would have been a good view, but I asked the soldiers about it, and they aren't allowed to go far unless they are armed and with a sergeant or officer. They do patrols and often lose a man. Not a nice place really, and the army patrols in Antigua are much the same."

The few days it took to go back to Anguilla passed quickly and on arrival both Merriman and Grahame visited the Governor. He had no further information for them, a situation which was repeated at St Kitts and Nevis. Arrival at Antigua was very different. The harbour was so packed with warships and transport vessels that *Aphrodite* had to anchor well offshore. As Merriman and Grahame were rowed ashore, they could see rows and rows of tents both on flat land and on the slopes above with groups of soldiers marching and performing what Merriman assumed were military exercises and training.

"Something serious is happening, James," commented Grahame, his voice muffled by a large kerchief he was holding to his nose in a vain effort not to breathe in the stench in the harbour.

He was right. On arrival at Admiral Howarth's offices they found the place filled with both army and naval officers discussing plans and a veritable army of clerks scribbling away on orders, lists of stores and all the multiplicity of forms needed to keep the navy afloat and the army organised.

They had to wait nearly an hour before they were told that the Admiral could see them. They were ushered into his private office to find even that room filled with senior officers including Colonel Shawcross. The Admiral, looking a little more than just harassed, welcomed them warmly, introductions were made, and he shouted for his servant to serve some refreshment. After the usual pleasantries, Colonel Shawcross was the first to speak.

"Captain Merriman, I have to tell you how pleased General Grey was to receive the information about the French in Martinique and St Lucia. He sent his warmest thanks to both you and Mr Grahame."

There were murmurs of agreement from the other officers. "Indeed yes, Captain, that should make our task much easier now we know what to expect," said Major James.

"Perhaps we should acquaint Captain Merriman with our plans, gentlemen. Would you, Colonel, like to begin with the army's part in all this?" said the Admiral. Again, nods and murmurs of agreement.

"Thank you, Admiral," said Shawcross. "As far as Martinique is concerned, General Grey plans the main attack from Barbados, arriving in Martinique on or around the fifth of February next year. There will be three main points of attack. The first will be in Galion Bay in the northeast and the second just north of Fort Royal Bay in the west and the third in the south-east of the island. The navy will supply covering fire to destroy or at least severely damage any forts and batteries they can see. Thanks to you two gentlemen we now know where most of them are. The two main forts guarding Fort Royal will have to be taken from the rear by direct assault."

"Thank you, Colonel, that is all very clear," said the Admiral. "From here we will send reinforcements and supplies, but we will not take part in the main assault, arriving just after. Captain Merriman and you Mr Grahame, will you want to go ashore to see if you can find any more of your agents?"

"Yes, sir, but I doubt I shall find many alive. They will have been caught by now as we have heard nothing from them since the French landed," replied Grahame. "But I must try."

"Of course you must, sir, and that means following the troops ashore as fast as possible. This brings me to another matter. Captain Merriman, I know you are not under my direct command but if you travel with the reinforcement ships we would be pleased if you would carry some of those reinforcements with you, otherwise some of those troops may have to be left behind."

"Yes, sir. Gladly, of course, but I will need to know exactly where to land them." As he said this, Merriman thought, *here we go again; more creeping round in the dark for Grahame, but that is what I brought him to the Indies to do.*

"Your orders will be given to you in due course, Captain, but it will be a few weeks yet. As you know, gentlemen, the Christmas season will be upon us in a few days so whilst we are all together, may I wish you all a happy Christmas and success in our endeavours."

Chapter Thirty-Eight

Christmas

Returning aboard, Merriman immediately called his officers to a meeting in his cabin. "Gentlemen," he said, "I must confess that I had completely forgotten about Christmas until I was reminded by the Admiral. I would like to suggest a big feast for all aboard. We should be able to buy ducks, chickens and geese ashore, maybe a big joint of beef and certainly a pig to butcher. We may have to have the beef roasted ashore somewhere. More vegetables and fruit would help. We shall have to go ashore, all of us, and see what we can find although I think all the ships in the harbour will have the same idea."

"Sir, sir, will we have decorations, sir?" asked young Oakley, jumping about with excitement.

"Yes, if we can, we'll have to buy ribbon, coloured cloth, paper, and such to make stars and bows and things. The men can do that if we find something suitable. Now you can all go ashore except the duty watch and see what we can buy but, before you go, wait while I tell the men."

"All hands, all hands on deck," bawled the bos'n, his mates and other petty officers.

The men poured up from below and gathered on deck, looking worriedly at each other, doubtless wondering what was wrong. First Lieutenant Laing shouted for silence and Merriman hoisted himself up onto the mizzen pin rail and waited until all were silent.

"Men, I have an important announcement to make," he said with a frown on his face. There was a shuffle of feet as the worried crew waited. Merriman waited a few moments longer and then with a broad smile said, "Men, it is Christmas in three days' time. It is my intention that we are going to celebrate. We shall have as big a feast as possible and decorations. Now if any of you have ideas, tell your petty officers who can tell me."

He stepped down to a roar of approval from the men who immediately started chattering excitedly. "Three cheers for the Cap'n lads. Hip, hip..." shouted a seaman from somewhere in the crowd, his voice drowned out by the noise of cheering.

"My word, gentlemen, I hope this event lives up to their expectations. It is up to us all to make it a good Christmas for them, and for us gentlemen," Merriman said. "I will go and see what can be obtained in the way of drink, ale, wine, and brandy from the hotel but if they have none for sale, they will direct me to somewhere it is available. I can find somebody to roast our beef as well. You can separate to find butchers, poulterers, and fruiterers and so on. You can take what is left of the money the governor sent aboard for the men but as I think this is all for the men, I think it is fair to use it. Now off you go and take some men with you to carry what you buy."

For two days the men in their spare time were involved with carving bits of wood and bone, cutting cloth and ribbon, and making dangling items of old bits of rope. On Christmas Eve the vegetables and fruit were stowed aboard and most of the meat was prepared, as were the birds, ready to cook in the morning. The cook had enlisted three men to help him and was swearing at them as he tried to make them understand what they had to do. A butcher had agreed to cook the beef starting early on Christmas Day, the wine and ale was aboard, and all seemed as ready as it could be by midnight.

The cook and his helpers were up well before dawn to start the cooking. Extra pans and cauldrons had been found from somewhere, exactly where Merriman dared not ask. The awnings and wind sails were rigged and after all the usual duties had been completed the men disappeared below to change into their best clothes. Merriman had given permission for the crew's mess tables and benches to be brought on deck and these quickly appeared covered with pieces of old sailcloth provided by the sailmaker. Merriman, his Officers, and Grahame and his uncle gathered in the great cabin for an aperitif and to discuss the details of the day. Merriman's servant, Peters, appeared with bottles of red wine and served it out.

"The man in the hotel recommended this one," said Merriman. "It is Spanish, but I can't get my tongue round the name."

"It's very good, sir," said Laing, a sentiment to which they all agreed.

Merriman had purchased a big box of cigars which he passed round, giving each of them a handful of the fine-smelling rolled tobacco leaf tubes. "These will go well with our after dinner brandy, gentlemen. If you, Charles, and you, Alfred, can't manage them, I'm sure somebody will buy them off you."

The two Midshipmen, somewhat amazed that their revered captain had unbent enough to use their given names, grinned and shuffled their feet. That the feast was now ready was signalled by the cook beating a spoon on a piece of old iron and Merriman's bos'n Owen appearing at the cabin door to announce it.

They all trooped up on deck to gather round Merriman's cabin table on the quarter deck to see the crew excitedly jostling for places at their tables. The cooks were ready, two men from each mess queuing up to collect the food with Peters at the front. A great shout for silence from Owen quieted everything as he announced, "The Captain will speak to you now."

Merriman rose to his feet. "As you know this is an unusual event on a ship of war, gentlemen, but as we have the opportunity I thought we should all relax today. I see the beef is coming aboard now so there is plenty to eat and drink but I warn you, if any man disgraces himself or his mess by over drinking and disgraceful behaviour he will find himself hauled up to the crosstrees. Do I make myself clear?"

"Aye-aye, sir. There'll be no trouble, sir," shouted several voices as the huge piece of beef, almost a whole carcass, was carried aboard by six sweating seamen and placed on rough table made by the carpenter.

Owen had joined Peters at the front of the queue and the cooks began to serve the food. There were joints of beef, lamb and pork, fish, and several whole chickens. Tubs of ale stood in the middle of each of the tables together with half a dozen bottles of wine. Merriman had specifically ordered that no rum was to be available until the regular evening tot.

Owen and Peters, together with two conscripted helpers, had secured two enormous trays which they heaped with some of all the different meats and vegetables and carried back to the officers on the quarterdeck. Silence descended as everybody tucked into the food and drink, trying some of the meats which some of them had never eaten before. The hush was broken by a lookout aloft shouting, "Deck there. Admiral's barge approaching, sir."

Frenzied activity took over. The bos'n and his mates together with the honour guard of marines - previously ordered by St James to hold themselves ready for such an eventuality - gathered by the entry port. The Officers had fled back to their quarters for their swords and hats and only just had time to be correctly dressed to welcome the Admiral.

Admiral Howarth climbed up on deck and raised his hat as the marines' presented arms and the whistles blew.

Merriman stepped forward. "It's a pleasure to welcome you aboard, sir. As you can see, we're having a bit of a party. May I ask you to join us?"

The Admiral looked round at the tables and at the food laid out. All the men were standing up, some of them chewing furiously and trying to hide the bones clutched in their hands.

"I think you should all sit down and continue your meal interrupted. Captain Merriman, I should be delighted to join you if you can find me a place."

Merriman asked Midshipman Oakley to give up his chair to the Admiral and whispered to him, "Have that lookout changed for another on the Rota. He can come down for his meal now." He turned to the Admiral. "Sir, may I recommend this Spanish wine, it is really very good."

Peters hastily found and filled another glass and gave it to the Admiral.

"By Jove, Captain, you're right, this really is good. Now then, introduce me to the officers I have not yet had the pleasure of meeting." That done, the Admiral selected a pile of meat and some vegetables and began to eat and drink as eagerly as the rest of them.

The cook had excelled himself and finally produced a prodigious duff, well soaked in brandy and that too was served out. Where he got the dried fruit from Merriman was afraid to ask.

Finally, the Admiral sat back, looked round him and said, "By Jove, Captain, I cannot remember when I have had a finer meal. Your cooks should be congratulated. We looked on from the flagship at all the activity, but I didn't expect all this, and the ship seems to be in excellent order as well. May I walk amongst your men and have a few words with them?"

"Of course, sir, I'll go round with you if you like."

"That won't be necessary, Captain. I've walked among seamen before." He picked up his hat and the officers watched in amazement as Admiral Howarth in all the finery of his full dress uniform, casually spoke to the men, plucked a chicken leg from a plate, and took a mug of ale that one of the men passed to him.

"You are lucky men, not many captains would have allowed this and so," he raised the mug and said, "a merry Christmas to you all." He drained the mug with one long swallow.

As he regained the quarterdeck a voice shouted "Three cheers for the Admiral lads –hip-hip…" The cheers rang out and the Admiral raised his hat in acknowledgement.

"Fine body of men you have, Captain, and now I must go back to my flagship. I thank you for an excellent and interesting meal and fine wine. It was a pleasure to meet you all, gentlemen, and you, Midshipman Oakley, thank you for giving up your chair. Goodbye, gentlemen."

Once the Admiral had departed, everyone seemed to relax. Little Oakley still sat in amazement. An Admiral had spoken to him and even knew his name. What a tale he would have to tell his family.

"Peters! More wine for everybody or brandy if they prefer but don't wake Mr Cuthbert, he is fast asleep."

Asleep he really was, and Merriman was reminded of the Christmas feasts at home and the rubicund Parson who always fell asleep at the table, not unusual in that age of excessive eating and drinking.

Merriman himself was beginning to find his eyes closing when a cough and a shuffling of feet behind him swiftly woke him up. "The men want to speak to you, sir, if you'll allow it," said Owen.

Merriman turned to find the whole crew standing quietly behind him. Merriman nodded and the ship's bos'n stepped forward. "Sir," he said, "the crew have elected me to speak for them. They want to thank you for all this food and wine you have arranged for them, and they wish you to accept this gift, sir. Jones Two, forward."

The marine stepped forward and gave Merriman a small polished wooden box with his name engraved on the top of the lid. *'Captain Merryman'*. He had to smile; his name had been spelt incorrectly. Opening it he found a beautifully made piece of scrimshaw work. A piece of bone carved and etched on one side to represent a cannon complete in every detail, and on the other side a ship in full sail, all the cuts picked out with lamp black he supposed. Merriman was taken aback as the crew cheered him and the officers applauded.

He stood up. "Men, I thank you all for this gift. I am pleased and flattered that you should think of it, and I know that some of you must have spent hours carving it. When I get home it will stand proudly on my desk. Again, I thank you all."

Another cheer and Merriman asked for the cook and his helpers to come forward. They stood in front of him, nervously, but he merely congratulated them and thanked them for their efforts and gave them all a drink of brandy. Normally at that time the servants and lower orders were treated as cattle, but Merriman's gesture had a big effect on the crew.

By that time darkness had almost fallen and the few lanterns the ship possessed were hung from the rigging to light up the deck and the men produced the various bits of decoration they had made. There were bows and tassels of bits of coloured cloth, and there were many small figures of children or dolls made from teased out oakum. These last had probably been made to remind men of the families they had left behind. A man produced a fiddle and began to play various melodies, sad ones that the crew listened to, some of them visibly moved at tunes that reminded them of home and all joining in to sing the usual sailor's songs. A young sailor began to sing of home and Merriman saw Oakley brush a surreptitious tear off his cheek. Even Mr Cuthbert had to sniff, clear his throat, and blow his nose.

    Merriman looked them over, his men, from different backgrounds, hard and rough, but his men, nevertheless. He was proud of them. Two sailors danced a hornpipe to the cheers of the others. He left the deck and turned into his cot, asleep almost immediately, never feeling Peters removing his shoes.

Chapter Thirty-Nine

Off to Martinique

The morning after the feast, Merriman was drifting in that delightful stage between dozing and being fully awake when he smelled coffee. He opened an eye to see Peters carrying a large jug of freshly brewed coffee. At the same time he became aware of the muffled curses of the warrant officers driving the men to work and some bumps and bangs as his table and chairs were carried down from the quarter deck into his cabin.

"Thank you, Peters, that is most welcome."

"Your breakfast is ready, sir. Some nice slices of chicken and a piece of pork. Shall I bring it, sir?" asked Peters.

"Yes, right away and then you can shave me and put out some clean clothes for me," replied the now fully awake Merriman.

When he was ready and wearing his best uniform and sword, he ascended the companion ladder to the deck. Lieutenants Laing and Andrews saluted him and apologised if the noise had wakened him. "Not at all, gentlemen, thank you. I'm pleased to see that most of the evidence of yesterday's festivity has disappeared."

"Yes, sir, we turned the men to at the first sign of daylight, the mess tables and benches are all back below, the decorations and empty bottles thrown overboard, and the men have almost finished with clearing and cleaning the deck."

Indeed, some of the men were still on their hands and knees busily scrubbing and using holystone to return the deck to its pristine whiteness. True, some of them wobbled a bit and had bloodshot eyes, but there was no sign of drunkenness.

"I'm pleased, gentlemen, to see the ship back to its usual condition. Tell me, were there any incidents last night that I should be aware of?"

"Nothing serious, sir. One or two men had a bit too much to drink but their mates carried them below and lashed them into their hammocks. They were desperate not to let you down after all you had done for them."

"Very good, Mr Laing. Will you tell them I want to see them in their divisions on deck at midday, all clean and respectable before I inspect the ship? Then they can assume the normal duties. I think another spell at sea will blow the cobwebs away and get the men to remember why they are here. I am going ashore now to see the Admiral for permission to sail."

Merriman had already told his cox'n Owen and his gig was already alongside, ready to take him ashore to see Admiral Howarth.

"Well, Captain, how are your ship and men this morning? A few thick heads I'll warrant."

"Yes, sir, but the men have been hard at work from daylight and the ship is clean again with no sign of the festivities to be seen. Ready for inspection if you care to see, sir."

"I don't think I need to, Captain, but tell me, were none of the men drunk and out of control?"

"One or two were, sir, but their mates quickly took them below and lashed them in their hammocks. You see, sir, I had threatened them with severe punishment if things got too bad. Everybody was well fed and had plenty to drink but they heeded my warning. And now, sir, the main reason I am here is to ask your permission to leave harbour tomorrow morning so that I can put my crew through enough exercises to be sure they are still as good as they were before we came here. Two or three days at the most should do."

"Permission granted, Captain. It is a capital idea and thank you again for that wonderful meal we had. How your cook and his helpers managed it all I don't know but it was far better than my cook could serve up."

"Thank you, sir. I don't know either, but I didn't dare ask."

Merriman returned to *Aphrodite,* carried out his promised inspection, made known his approval and then informed his officers that the ship would sail at dawn on the next day. Thus, it was that the ship spent a fruitful three days at sea with the officers putting the men through all that they knew, starting them shortening sail then a few minutes later before that was done, Merriman changed his mind and ordered them to do something else.

The men practised lowering yards and then swaying them up again, changing the tiller ropes in case they were damaged. He had the marine drummer beat to quarters for battle and the guns loaded but unshotted, then fired. This practice was repeated and repeated and then he had the men prepare for what to do if one or two of the gun crews were killed. He had several men carried below all at once, supposedly injured so that McBride the surgeon could practice with his helpers what they would have to do when the real thing happened. In the middle of all that he ordered course changes repeatedly.

He worked them hard, both day and night, giving them only short breaks for food of which there was still plenty. On the morning of the third day Merriman had them all practice moving the guns round from side to side with all men including the officers sweating hard. Captain Merriman himself, stood with his timepiece in hand until he announced himself satisfied.

Lieutenant Laing came to him and said, "I had no idea how far the men had fallen behind their usual times for carrying out the orders, sir, but I'm pleased to report that they are now as good as or even better than before. Some of the men were grumbling but I heard the bos'n sharply reminding them that all the work might save their lives one day."

No sooner had *Aphrodite* dropped anchor in the afternoon of that third day, when Shrigley the signals Midshipman shouted out, "Signal from Flag, sir. Our number. Captain to report to Flag immediately."

It was expected and Merriman was ready in his best uniform to go to the Flagship. Admiral Howarth greeted him warmly, offered a drink and then asked if the last three days had been successful.

"Oh yes, sir, no doubt about it. When we left here I could see that some of the men needed sharpening up a bit, but I worked them hard and I'm happy to say that now they are as good as ever," replied Merriman.

"Glad to hear it, Captain. Our orders have arrived from General Grey and Admiral Jervis in Barbados. Both his fleet and his transport vessels are to meet ours west of Martinique on the fourth of next month prepared to start the assault at dawn on the fifth. We are to carry his reinforcements so fifty men of the 22nd regiment will join you and you must practice getting them ashore and back by boat, regardless of the state of the sea. The other ships are doing the same as we speak. The troops will sleep ashore until we move out for Martinique. Is that all clear? Good, here are your written orders."

Once again Merriman called his officers to his cabin to tell them what the orders entailed. Plenty of practice would be needed to get clumsy soldiers in and out of the boats, which most of them would not have done before.

"I bet some of them fall in," said Andrews with a grin on his face.

"Very likely, David, so men must be ready to fish them out," answered Merriman.

In the event the practice went well. Only two soldiers fell out of the boats and were dragged back aboard soaking wet, embarrassed and the butt of the other men's ribald jokes.

Chapter Forty

The attack on Martinique

On the morning of the fifth of January, the action was opened by the two deck seventy-fours and the bigger three deck ships opening a barrage on all the forts and batteries they could see above the carefully picked places where the troops would land. That didn't take long, and French soldiers could be seen running for their lives as the fortifications tumbled around them.

The British soldiers were quickly put on shore where they wasted no time in dealing with French stragglers. General Grey and two thousand five hundred of his men landed at the southern end of the island west of St Lucia and advanced over difficult and mountainous roads to a place called Rivière-Salée.

Two other almost unopposed landings were made at the same time at the bay of Galion in the northeast of Martinique and also north of Fort Royal Bay in the west. General Grey dispatched men to attack the batteries on Cape Solomon and Point Bourges from the rear. That was carried out almost bloodlessly, the French putting up only a feeble defence. It was not long before the three sets of attacking troops had almost encircled the island's capital Fort Royal and the commanders could see the next forts to be assaulted.

The two big forts, Fort Royal and Bourbon, were situated to command the harbour and its approaches and would not be so easily taken. Both were strongly built and well garrisoned, so batteries were erected against them and the town of Port Royal. Eventually both were taken by direct and bloody attack. At the point of the bayonet, the commandant and the town capitulated.

While all that was going on, Merriman and *Aphrodite* were carrying out their orders, assisting in putting men and the supplies the army needed ashore. They took no part in any fighting and grumbles were heard that they weren't allowed to fight. However, once the fighting ceased, British ships anchored in the harbour including the *Aphrodite,* and Grahame and his uncle went ashore with a guard of marines. Seated in a small, commandeered cart, they set off for the Grahame estate.

It was in a mess, the buildings burned and the sugar crushing mill so badly damaged as to need a total rebuilding.

"It's no good, Laurence," said the older man. "I can't afford to buy more slaves to rebuild it although I don't think I have the energy to tackle it if I had. I have been thinking hard about what I can do and if you could arrange it I think I would like to go back to England, there may be some family there. But before we go I must find your Aunt Rachael's grave, and see what state it is in. It's over there beneath that big tree."

The site was completely overgrown, and Grahame had to ask the marines to use their bayonets to clear a path. The two men stood in silence looking at the destruction. What had been a neat and tidy grave was as much of a mess as the house. The headstone, once in the shape of a cross, had been thrown on its back and smashed into fragments.

"What kind of people would do this?" asked the older man brokenly.

"I don't know, Uncle, but we can't do anything about it now. Hello, here's a piece of the stone with the name Rachael on it on it. You could keep that if you like."

The old man nodded and fell to his knees in prayer beside the ruined grave. Grahame and the marines waited patiently until he had finished and then lifted him to his feet.

"I think we should go now, Uncle. I'll take you and the stone back to the ship where you can rest."

In the cart drawn by a half-starved horse the old man finally broke down and simply sat there with tears rolling down his face. "We were so happy here once, Laurence, and now it's all gone except the memories." At that thought, he brightened a little. "At least I still have those."

Back at the ship, some of the marines took the man aboard and told Merriman what had happened.

"Better take him down to Mr McBride, men, he will look after him. Where is Mr Grahame now?" Merriman asked.

"He took the cart an' three of us as a guard and set off to see if he could find any of 'is agents, sir. 'E didn't say how long 'e would be, sir," said one of the men.

"I see, anyway thank you for bringing Mr Grahame back."

It was after dark when Grahame and his guard came back aboard. "It's no good, James," he told Merriman. "I couldn't find any of the people I knew although I was told that three of them had been shot by the French."

Peters appeared with a jug of steaming coffee and two mugs.

"Peters, you are a life saver, I needed this. The marines and I haven't eaten all day and I'm famished. Could some food be found for us?"

Merriman nodded and Peters disappeared.

Chapter Forty-One

News from home

Over the next six or eight weeks, St Lucia and Guadeloupe were taken by General Grey's forces with almost complete success. St Lucia was taken quickly thanks in a large part to the information supplied by Grahame and his agent Briggs who had died to get it. Guadeloupe took longer as no information about the French defences had been obtained. In the harbours there, more privateers were found, mostly short of replacement rope and canvas. They were burned except for two of the best which the navy took as prizes.

In all cases after the attacks Grahame had to be taken round the islands to try and find any of his agents who may still be alive. But it was a fruitless task, only one or two were found and they wanted no more to do with the business. Back in Merriman's cabin, Grahame almost stamped his feet in frustration and annoyance.

"It's no good, James. I shall have to start all over again to find suitable people and that could take months or more."

And so began several weeks sailing round the recently captured islands and most of the other islands still occupied by either French or Spanish forces. This of course involved night landings by Grahame with *Aphrodite* dropping him ashore and picking him up again one or two or even more days later. The quest continued for months, broken only by the ship returning to Antigua or Barbados for supplies of food and water. In Jamaica they picked up Grahame's uncle who was very relieved to be back on board.

During all this time Grahame became more and more exhausted, ill, and refused to eat until Merriman stepped in and refused to take him anywhere else until he had recovered. Of course, he objected, but as Merriman said, "You are worn out, sir. Your efforts have so far have had no success and I don't want to have to report to Lord Stevenage that I had to bury you at sea."

Grahame reluctantly acquiesced and they returned yet again to Antigua. Here they found out that the Naval Postal Service had caught up with them, bringing orders and letters for both of them and also letters for the officers and a surprising number for the crew. Eagerly, Merriman opened his letters. Two were from his father recording family affairs and two more were from his bride in waiting, Helen. He read them time and time again. She told him how much she missed him and longed for his return. Her father Doctor Simpson was well and sent his regards, and after all the trivia she told him how much she loved him and that she was longing for his embrace. The letter finished with more endearments which he certainly wanted no one else to read.

He strode about the deck smiling from ear to ear while his men grinned and whispered to each other, "Captain's 'ad good news likely an' good luck to 'im." The mood of the whole ship lightened. Men were in odd corners reading their letters, or having them read to them, but inevitably some men had none and they wandered round with long faces.

Grahame came on deck to find Merriman, saying, "James, I have orders to go up the east coast of America and to Washington to find out the mood of the people after Independence and, if possible, to learn something about any of their government plans which might affect England. On the way we must call in at as many ports as we can looking for privateers. The American Government has banned French and Spanish privateers from its ports, but we are to find out if that ban is working."

"Very well, sir. I look forward to finding cooler weather up north."

Merriman summoned his officers, instructing them to make preparations for the onward voyage.

THE END

Homeward bound

From here the narrative must be somewhat sketchy. As noted in the foreword to this book, many of the Merriman papers and letters had been destroyed by damp and vermin and try as we could, little more could be learned.

It seems that the ship moved north ending up near Boston. Grahame was ordered home and left the ship to report to the Treasury. While he said he would be back, Merriman was left behind because he had no orders to take Grahame home. By then he had been away from home for over three years.

Because he was nominally under the orders of Grahame, who was no longer there, he and his ship were appropriated by the Admiral in command of the Navy. They were ordered to act as convoy escort up and down the eastern side of America without returning home. Finally, he received orders from the Admiralty to return home 'with all dispatch'. By the time he reached England, some years had passed since leaving home.

We learn no more until the events used for the writing of the next novel, The French Invasion, came to light.

Author Biography
Roger Burnage (1933 to 2015)

Roger Burnage had an eventful life that ultimately led him to pursue his passion for writing. Born and raised in the village of Lymm, Warrington, Cheshire, United Kingdom, he embarked on a journey of adventure and self-discovery.

Roger's life took an intriguing turn when he served in the Royal Air Force (RAF) during his national service. He was stationed in Ceylon, which is now known as Sri Lanka, where he worked as a radio mechanic, handling large transmitters.

After his release from the RAF, Roger went on to work as a draughtsman at Vickers in Manchester. Through dedication and hard work, he eventually climbed the ranks to become a sales engineer. His job involved traveling abroad to places like Scandinavia and India, which exposed him to new cultures and experiences.

It was during this period that Roger Burnage stumbled upon the Hornblower novels by C. S. Forester. The captivating tales of naval adventures ignited a spark of interest in the historical fiction genre within him.

Eventually, Roger settled in North Wales, where he focused on building a business and raising a family. Throughout his professional and personal life, the desire to write for himself never waned. However, it wasn't until retirement that he finally had the time and opportunity to pursue his dream of becoming an author.

Despite facing initial challenges and enduring multiple rejections from publishers and agents, Roger persevered. He refused to give up on his writing aspirations. Even when he underwent open-heart surgery and had an operation for a brain haemorrhage, he continued to work diligently on his craft. Typing away with only two fingers for months on end, he crafted "The Merriman Chronicles."

In 2012, with the support of his youngest son, Robin, Roger self-published his debut novel, "A Certain Threat," on Amazon KDP, making it available in both paperback and Kindle formats. His determination and talent began to bear fruit, as his fan base grew, and book sales remained strong.

More information about
The Merriman Chronicles is available online

Follow the Author on Amazon

Get notified when a new books and audiobooks are released.

Desktop, Mobile & Tablet:
Search for the author, click the author's name on any of the book pages to jump to the Amazon author page, click the follow button at the bottom.

Kindle eReader and Kindle Apps:
The follow button is normally after the last page of the book.

Don't forget to leave a review or rating too!

For more background information, book details and announcements of upcoming novels, check the website at:

www.merriman-chronicles.com

You can also follow us on social media:-

https://twitter.com/Merriman1792

https://www.facebook.com/MerrimanChronicles

Printed in Great Britain
by Amazon